snatched!

Brian got into the car and Roni took off, wheels spinning.

"How come you're running around loose, Stink Bomb?" she asked. "Didn't your parents put you under house arrest?"

"My name's not Stink Bomb. It's Brian."

"Really? You don't *look* like a Brian."

"What's that supposed to mean?"

"I mean, you look like a Quincy. Or maybe a Hector, or a Zigmund. I expected you to have a really weird name, like a mad scientist. You being a mad stink bomber and all."

Brian said, "I'll probably be grounded when my mom gets home, but my dad's clueless. How about you?"

"I'm going over to Alicia's to make the big apology. One way to get out of the house. Maybe she'll be cool and talk to me about what happened."

"I doubt it," Brian said.

"You don't have to be so negative."

"Well, I'm pretty sure about this. Alicia just got snatched."

OTHER SLEUTH BOOKS YOU MAY ENJOY

THE BLOODWATER MYSTERIES

snatched

**PETE HAUTMAN
AND MARY LOGUE**

Ellington Middle School
Library Media Center

SLEUTH
PUFFIN

PUFFIN BOOKS

Published by the Penguin Group

Penguin Young Readers Group, 345 Hudson Street, New York, New York 10014, U.S.A.

Penguin Group (Canada), 90 Eglinton Avenue East, Suite 700,
Toronto, Ontario, Canada M4P 2Y3 (a division of Pearson Penguin Canada Inc.)

Penguin Books Ltd, 80 Strand, London WC2R 0RL, England

Penguin Ireland, 25 St Stephen's Green, Dublin 2, Ireland
(a division of Penguin Books Ltd)

Penguin Group (Australia), 250 Camberwell Road, Camberwell, Victoria 3124, Australia
(a division of Pearson Australia Group Pty Ltd)

Penguin Books India Pvt Ltd, 11 Community Centre,
Panchsheel Park, New Delhi - 110 017, India

Penguin Group (NZ), 67 Apollo Drive, Mairangi Bay, Auckland 1311, New Zealand
(a division of Pearson New Zealand Ltd)

Penguin Books (South Africa) (Pty) Ltd, 24 Sturdee Avenue,
Rosebank, Johannesburg 2196, South Africa

Registered Offices: Penguin Books Ltd, 80 Strand, London WC2R 0RL, England

First published in the United States of America by G. P. Putnam's Sons,
a division of Penguin Young Readers Group, 2006
This Sleuth edition published by Puffin Books,
a division of Penguin Young Readers Group, 2007

1 3 5 7 9 10 8 6 4 2

THE LIBRARY OF CONGRESS HAS CATALOGED
THE G. P. PUTNAM'S SONS /SLEUTH EDITION AS FOLLOWS:

Hautman, Pete, date. Snatched / Pete Hautman and Mary Logue. p. cm.—
(The Bloodwater mysteries) Summary: Too curious for her own good, Roni,
crime reporter for her high school newspaper, teams up with Brian,
freshman science geek, to investigate the beating and kidnapping of a classmate.
[1. Reporters and reporting—Fiction. 2. Kidnapping—Fiction.
3. Mystery and detective stories.]
I. Logue, Mary. II. Title. III. Series: Hautman, Pete, date .
The Bloodwater mysteries. PZ7. H2887Sn 2006 [Fic]—dc22 2005028558
ISBN 0-399-24377-1 (hc)

Puffin/Sleuth ISBN 978-0-14-240795-0

Printed in the United States of America

For Tucker

contents

1

poison honey

Alicia watched the blood drip from her nose to the grass. She was on her hands and knees, hair covering her face like a veil. The blood looked black in the fading light of dusk.

Funny. It didn't even hurt.

What would she look like in the morning?

She heard his voice, like poisoned honey. "Alicia?"

"Leave me alone!" Her voice sounded wrong. Her lips felt thick and mushy.

"Are you okay, sweetie?"

She said nothing. He knew she wasn't okay. He knew everything. He even knew what would happen next. She would clean herself up, and tomorrow she would make up some story and they would pretend it had never happened.

She lied all the time. Sometimes she didn't even know what was true anymore. She lived in two worlds and sometimes they were the same, but more often they were different. One world was light and airy, the other was dark and scary.

He touched her shoulder. She swung her arm and knocked his hand aside.

"Go away!" she shouted.

He was standing over her. She could see the tips of his shoes. She closed her eyes. She could hear him breathing.

And then, after what seemed a long time, she heard his footsteps fading away.

She touched her hand to her face, then looked at it. Her fingers were dark with blood, but she felt no pain. She never did anymore. But this time it was bad. She had never before been hit so hard. Her face would be a mess.

How would she explain it this time?

2

girl talk

*Last Friday a Bloodwater High student was
mysteriously attacked and left for dead in
Riverfront Park.*

*The victim, Alicia Camden, was found dazed
and bleeding near the park entrance. She was
taken to Mercy Hospital and treated for cuts and
bruises, and for being scared half to death.*

*Although she has lived in Bloodwater only since
the beginning of this school year, Alicia is a
member of the tennis team, and lead actress in
the school production of The Crucible. She is
admired and well liked by all, which makes the
reason for this unprovoked attack extremely bizarre.*

*Since the unfortunate and nearly tragic incident,
students are advised to carry large handguns
and shoot all strangers on sight.*

Roni frowned at what she had written in her notebook. Not
exactly a triumph of investigative reporting. In fact, it was
pretty much what had been printed in the local newspaper
that weekend, with a few embellishments. She needed a fresh
angle, and it had to be good. It wasn't every day she had a real
crime to report.

Roni was sitting in the warm autumn sun on the steps in front of Bloodwater High School, along with several other students. Most of them were eating their lunch. Roni did not eat lunch. She had given it up in an effort to lose weight. So far, it wasn't working.

She scowled at her notebook, trying not to think about food, and made a few changes in her story. She crossed out the words "left for dead," and "well liked by all." The first was probably not true, since the injuries hadn't been that severe—it was only Monday, and Alicia was already back in school. As for the second item, Alicia was not terrifically popular. She was involved in plenty of school activities, but she didn't seem to have a lot of friends. This made Roni like her better, not being terrifically popular herself.

Alicia did, however, have a boyfriend, Maurice Wellington. Maurice was the star of the basketball team, and one of the best-looking guys in school.

Roni left in the bit about "shoot all strangers on sight." Roni always made it a point to give Mr. Spindler, the school principal, something to delete.

She was making a few more changes in her article when an attractive blond girl wearing oversize sunglasses and carrying a lime green designer backpack over her shoulder came through the front doors and trotted down the steps.

Roni jumped to her feet. "Hey Alicia!"

Alicia Camden stopped at the bottom of the steps and looked back. She waited for Roni to catch up to her.

"Got a minute?" Roni asked.

Alicia was wearing a lot of makeup, but not enough to cover the cut on her lip.

"Not really," she said. "My mom's picking me up for a doctor appointment." She stared at Roni through her sunglasses. "Do I know you?"

"My name's Roni. Listen, I heard about what happened to you."

"You and everybody else in the galaxy."

"How are you feeling?"

Alicia lifted her sunglasses to reveal a huge purple and yellow bruise around her right eye. "How does it look like I feel?"

"Kind of not so great," Roni said.

"Thanks a lot." Alicia lowered her glasses and started walking away.

"Wait a sec." Roni fell in beside her. "I was wondering if I could talk to you about what happened."

"Why? Are you some sort of accident geek?"

"Actually, I'm an investigator for the *Bloodwater Pump*."

"The *Pump*?" Alicia laughed. "The school newspaper?"

"That's right."

"The police don't want me to talk to reporters. Not even for that little rag."

Little rag? Roni felt her blood pressure rise. "Why not?"

"Because."

"Because why?"

"Because they don't want anybody to mess up their investigation, that's why."

"Did you see who hit you?"

"No. It was dark. Look, I told you, I'm not supposed to talk to reporters."

"Do the police have any suspects at all?"

Alicia stopped and turned on Roni. "You're kind of pushy, aren't you?"

"I'm a reporter," said Roni. "It's what I do."

"Well, why don't you do it someplace else. I gotta go. My mom's here." She pointed at the SUV parked at the curb. The woman behind the wheel looked like an older version of Alicia—thin, blond, stylish, and snooty. Even their hairstyles were the same.

Alicia's mom leaned on her horn. Alicia turned away from Roni and started for the car.

"Wait . . ." Roni reached out and grabbed Alicia's elbow.

"I said leave me ALONE!" Alicia whirled, swinging her backpack. Roni saw it coming, but not in time. The heavy pack hit her in the chest and knocked her backward. She landed hard on her butt.

"Hey!" Roni scrambled to her feet, her heart pounding. She felt herself losing control. Even as a little voice inside her said, Count to ten, girl, she was charging at Alicia, who was walking away as if nothing had happened.

Roni grabbed Alicia's backpack, saying, "Wait a minute!"

Alicia turned and pushed Roni, but Roni didn't let go of her backpack. They both toppled and fell to the ground. Alicia let out a shriek and kicked at Roni's head, but this time

Roni was ready for her—she ducked the kick and rolled on top of Alicia, pinning her arms to the sidewalk.

"I just wanted to ask you a couple of questions!" she shouted.

That was when Alicia really started yelling.

3.

suspended

"Do you know what 'zero tolerance' means?" asked Mr. Spindler.

"I was just . . . ," Roni said.

Spindler cut her off. "Wrong answer. Zero tolerance means that this school will not abide violence of any sort. It means that *any* fighting will be dealt with harshly."

"Then you should deal with Alicia—she attacked me."

"We will talk with Alicia—but don't you think that poor girl has gone through enough in the past few days?"

"That's why I had to talk to her. I was just asking her a few questions and all of a sudden she hits me with her backpack."

"Roni, Roni, Roni," said Mr. Spindler, shaking his head. "What are we going to do with you? Last time we had this problem you said it was because some boy called you names."

"Justin Riverwood called me Thunderthighs. And I didn't hit him, I just poured a Coke over his head."

"And the time before that?"

"You mean the time Krista Rose stole my Walkman?"

"I mean the time you broke into Krista Rose's locker with a crowbar."

Roni shrugged. That was all ancient history. "The point is," she said, "I was working on an official news story for the

Pump, and I asked Alicia a couple of legitimate questions, and she hit me with her backpack. It's a clear case of self-defense."

"That is not what Alicia's mother said, Roni."

"Look, all I did was grab her backpack. Then she tries to kick me and starts hollering like some psycho killer's got her. My ears are still ringing."

"Yes, well, in any case, you were fighting on school property, and that's a mandatory four-day suspension. We've called your mother to pick you up. Until then, you will wait outside in the office."

"That's not fair."

"I didn't say it was."

"What about Alicia? Is she suspended, too?" Roni asked as she left the office.

Spindler didn't bother to answer.

4

the stench

Brian Bain hated The Bench.

Spindler had left him sitting on that incredibly hard wooden bench outside his office for nearly half an hour. There wasn't a lot to do on The Bench. Except listen to Mrs. Washington type on her computer. Or read the school newspaper, the *Bloodwater Pump*. It was all part of the punishment, Brian figured, which was completely not fair, on account of nothing had actually happened yet.

He flipped through the paper—all four pages of it. Football . . . boring. Debate Club . . . borrrring. Fund-raiser for girls' hockey . . . BORRRRRRing. He turned to the back page to read the "Crime Corner," a column by P. Q. Delicata. Sometimes that was pretty interesting. You never knew what sort of strange criminal activity P.Q. was going to report on next. Even when nothing much bad had happened, P.Q. knew how to make it sound interesting.

> Crime is running rampant at Bloodwater High this week. Tiffany Danielson reports the brazen theft of a Lisa Simpson magnet from the front of her locker.
>
> "Hey, it only cost me ninety-nine cents," Tiffany said, "but it had sentimental value."

Anyone with knowledge of this or other magnet misappropriations should report it directly to the FBI.

Speaking of sentimental value, Jim Hall's infamous 1983 Dodge Aries was viciously keyed in the school parking lot, causing a massive rearrangement of rust molecules and terrible personal anguish for Mr. Hall. "I don't know why, but ever since it got scratched, it's burning twice as much oil as before," he said.

Witnesses to the keying should follow the cloud of blue exhaust smoke to Mr. Hall and report their findings.

Aside from the criminal horrors listed above, it's been a quiet week in Bloodwater. No terrorist activity, vampire attacks, train robberies, or ritual beheadings have reached this reporter's sensitive ears.

Brian liked the way P. Q. Delicata wrote. He was still reading when Spindler's door opened and a girl came out and sat down next to him.

Spindler stuck his head out of his office, looked at Brian, and sighed. "Not you again, Bain!"

Brian smiled and shrugged.

Spindler put on his holy martyr face. Looking back and forth from Brian to the girl, he said, "What did I ever do to deserve you two?" When neither of them answered, he sighed and said, "I'll deal with you in a few minutes, Mr. Bain. In the meantime, try not to blow anything up, okay?" He closed his door.

Oh well. Brian was in no hurry to get reamed out by Spindler. He looked at the girl sitting next to him. She was wearing a big, thick sweater and baggy jeans. Her hair was long and straight, and she sat kind of hunched over at the shoulders. She was older than Brian, probably in eleventh grade. A small silver ring decorated her left nostril. Her other nostril sported a medium-size zit, which she had tried to cover up with makeup. Except for the zit and the way she dressed, she wasn't bad looking. He decided that she rated a seven on a scale of one to ten.

She had sat down right in the middle of the bench, about fifteen inches away from him. It was a long bench. She didn't have to sit that close, as if she didn't even know he was there. And she looked mad. *Really* mad, like her eardrums were about to pop.

Not wanting to be too close when her brain exploded, Brian scooted over a few inches.

That got her attention.

"What are you gawking at?" She looked at him as if he were a bug.

Brian looked straight back at her. One thing he had learned about older kids was that if you look right in their eyes, they respect you more. Either that or they hit you.

"Nothing," he said.

"Good." She turned her glare on the floor a few feet in front of her clunky black boots.

They sat without saying anything for about two minutes, which was a long time to sit on such a hard bench doing nothing. Brian decided to ask her a question.

"What are you in for?"

She didn't lift her head to talk. Didn't even turn her head. She kept staring at the floor.

"I'm an investigator," she said. "I was doing my job."

That sounded interesting. His mother was an investigator, too. Brian liked to think it ran in the family.

"What were you investigating?"

"The Camden case. Not that it's any of your business." She squinted at him. "Aren't you a little young to be in high school?"

"I'm fourteen," Brian said, adding a few months to his real age. "I got bumped up a grade."

"Child prodigy, huh?"

"Not really. What's the Camden case? Is that about the girl that got beat up?"

She nodded.

"My mom's working on that one," Brian said.

She looked at him. "Your mom?"

"Yeah. She's a cop."

"A real cop?"

"No. An imitation plastic cop." He tensed up, bracing

himself. After making a sarcastic comment, it was a good idea to be ready for anything.

But instead of being offended, the girl said, "I like the plastic kind. They're very durable." She paused, then asked, "Your mom is really working on the Camden case?"

"She's the lead detective for the Bloodwater police."

"Do they have any suspects?"

"I don't know. She doesn't talk about her work much. What sort of investigator are you, anyway?"

"I work for the *Pump*."

"Wait a second . . . are *you* P. Q. Delicata?"

"Yeah," she said. "But you can call me Roni."

"I like your column," he said.

For the first time, Brian saw her smile. She had a good one.

"Thanks," she said. "What's your name?"

Before Brian could answer, Spindler opened his door. "Okay, Mr. Bain. It's your turn." He went back to his desk, leaving the door open for Brian.

"He doesn't seem to like you," said Roni in a low voice. "What did you do?"

"Unauthorized use of the chem lab," Brian said, standing up. "No big deal—except I got interrupted before I could finish my experiment." He grimaced. "I just hope old Bismuth had the sense to turn off that Bunsen burner."

Just then the office door flew open and Mrs. Bismuth, the chemistry teacher, staggered in, red-faced and pop-eyed. She slammed the door behind her and let out her breath in a long, ragged gasp, as if she'd been holding it for minutes. "It's *horrible,*" she said, coughing.

"What? What's wrong?" said Mrs. Washington.

"Horrible," was all Mrs. Bismuth could say.

Brian became aware of a faint, familiar, ferociously foul odor that quickly increased in intensity. They heard people running in the hall, and sounds of gagging, and then the door burst open again and several students ran in followed by a wave of stink so unutterably dreadful that even P. Q. Delicata could not have begun to describe it. The stench rolled over them like an invisible wave of rotten eggs, ancient sewage, and dead skunk.

Just then, Mrs. Bismuth spotted Brian. She pointed a shaking finger at him and said in a choked voice, "You! This is all your fault!"

5

ride

Standing on the sidewalk outside the hospital wearing her mother's oversize sunglasses, Alicia felt as if she were invisible. She could stand there for days and no one would notice her. Just another teenage girl.

During Alicia's follow-up appointment in the hospital, Dr. Chao had been very kind. She had held Alicia's face in her hands and gently touched the bruises.

"How scary it must have been," Dr. Chao had said. "Why would someone do that?"

Alicia had felt like crying for the first time since the incident. She had wanted to tell this gentle woman with the dark-rimmed glasses all about her life, but she didn't dare. Instead she had dropped her head and mumbled something about still not remembering what had happened.

"That isn't unusual," Dr. Chao had said. "Memories might come back to you. You'll need to talk about it eventually."

Alicia's mom hadn't come in with her. She had just dropped her off at the front door. She had errands to run. More important things to do. Dr. Chao hadn't said anything, but she had seemed surprised when Alicia came in all by herself.

"Your bruises are healing nicely," Dr. Chao had said, smiling. "I don't think we'll need to see you again, Alicia."

All by herself. It didn't used to be that way. When she had lived in Mankato—before her mother had divorced and remarried—she'd had friends. She'd had a real father. But here in Bloodwater everything was different.

And now her mom was twenty minutes late to pick her up.

Alicia looked around. Nobody cared. Two orderlies smoking cigarettes on a bus bench. An old man helping an old woman with a cane. A little kid in a wheelchair. Alicia stared down at her feet. Nobody even knew she was alive.

An SUV pulled over to the curb in front of her.

"Need a lift?"

Alicia raised her eyes and looked in at the driver.

6

bovine pustules

Brian stood in the doorway of his father's study. The room looked as if a tornado had hit it. That was normal. Books covered the floor, the chairs, the desk. The shiny top of his father's balding head could be seen above the waves of books, but only because his father was very tall.

Bruce Bain was a not-famous author. He wrote strange, intelligent books that got great reviews, but that only a few strange, intelligent people read. His books had titles like *Bivalves of the Upper Mississippi,* and *Narcissistic Behavior in Flatworms.* Recently, he had been working on something called *The Entomology of Bovine Pustules.*

Brian had tried to read his father's books. They made him feel as if his brain were crumbling.

But then, his father couldn't even balance his own checkbook. Neither could his mother. Brian had been doing it for them since he was ten.

"Hey, Dad," Brian said in a quiet voice. His father had been known to jump straight up out of his chair when startled.

This time he levitated only a few inches.

"Huh? What?" He peered over the mountain of books. "Ah! Brian. Home so soon? How are you, son?"

"Fine, Dad."

"Good, good."

"I got suspended from school."

His father smiled hazily. "School. Yes. Good. Hmm. And how is school going?"

"Wellll . . . my hydrogen sulfide generator got left on. It wasn't my fault."

"Hydrogen sulfide." He blinked. "Very smelly, yes. Major component of intestinal gases, hmm, uh-huh, yes . . . cattle create a great deal of it."

"They had to evacuate the school."

"Yes, well, I'm glad to hear it. Good work, son."

Brian was sure that nothing he had said had penetrated. His father's head was still deep in *The Entomology of Bovine Pustules.* That was fine with him.

"Well, I gotta go snazzledorf my finkwalter."

"I see, well, that's nice, son. I'm glad you had a good day at school."

"Thanks, Dad."

His father's head sank beneath the ocean of books.

"When's Mom coming home? I need to ask her about a case she's working on."

He was interrupted by the horrible clatter of his father's antique rotary dial telephone.

Brian's father hated telephones above all things on earth. He shuffled through the books and papers on his desk, searching for the source of the ringing. Brian thought about running and answering the kitchen extension, but he was curious how long it would take his father to find his phone.

It took ten rings.

"Hello? Oh, hello, dear."

It had to be his mother. Brian listened to one end of the conversation.

"Yes. Oh. That's awful. Oh dear. Oh my. That's very bad. Yes, no, yes, don't worry about us, dear. We'll just whip something up. Okay. Bye now."

Brian heard the click of the phone being set back in its cradle, then a sigh, then the soft clatter of typing.

"Dad?"

His father's head popped up.

"Brian? Back so soon?"

"I never left. Was that Mom?"

"Yes. She's going to be running late this evening."

"So is it tuna melt sandwiches for dinner again?" Tuna melt was the only thing his father knew how to make.

"I'm afraid so. She might be quite late. Apparently, something terrible has happened to one of your classmates."

7

meat loaf

"Nick, you're looking at this the entirely wrong way. Think of it as a time for me to find myself."

Roni's mother, Nicoletta Delicata, better known as Nick, was attempting to make dinner. Roni stared at the mess her mother was mashing together in a big yellow bowl. Nick was not a great cook. They ate grilled cheese sandwiches and tomato soup so often that Roni was thinking of buying stock in Campbell's. But for tonight Nick was making something she claimed was "meat loaf."

"You've been suspended from school for a week. How else can I look at it?"

"It's not a week. It's four days."

"That's hardly the point. I'm very disappointed in you, Petronella." She stopped attacking the meat loaf mixture for a moment and pointed her wooden spoon at Roni.

"You are grounded. You are cleaning the house from top to bottom. You are keeping up with your schoolwork. The television is moving to my room and your laptop will be used for homework only for the next month."

Roni didn't like what she was hearing.

Then her mother severed the final line of communication with the outside world. "No phone."

Roni whined and moaned. She knew that was what her

mother expected. She didn't point out how impossible it would be for her mother to enforce these new rules while she was at work all day long. As the mayor's secretary, Nick took her job very seriously. The mayor, Buddy Berglund, spent most of his time on the golf course, so she had to make most of his decisions for him. In effect, Nick Delicata ran the city of Bloodwater.

"Whatever were you thinking, fighting with a fellow student?"

"I was investigating," Roni said.

"Oh, so now you resort to beating information out of people?"

"I already told you. She started it."

"Yes, I did hear that part. And what should you have done?"

"I just wanted her to listen to me. She acted like I was some pesky fly that she could swat away."

Roni saw a small smile land on her mother's lips for a moment. "Well, sometimes you are pesky."

"I know. But now I won't get anything out of her. I don't mind the suspension, but this is a big story."

"Maybe you should apologize," her mother suggested.

"But I didn't do anything wrong!"

"Saying you're sorry never hurts."

At first Roni thought her mother's suggestion was ridiculous. But then she thought about it more. A reason to go over to Alicia's house. Her mother couldn't object—she had suggested it.

"She lives at the old Bloodwater place, all the way over by the park," Roni said. "Can I use the car?"

"I was thinking you could simply use the phone."

"I thought the phone was off limits."

"In this case, I would make an exception."

"I think it would be better if I apologized in person. I could drive over there right now."

Nick frowned at her daughter, then shrugged. "All right, but I don't want you gallivanting off on any of your auxiliary adventures, dear. This is a onetime exception—you are still grounded."

Things were looking up. Roni told Nick about the other thing that had happened that day. "Some kid had a chemistry experiment go stink bomb today. They evacuated the school. So actually I'm suspended only for three days, since everybody got out early today anyway."

"That sounds dangerous," Nick said. "Were there toxic gases?"

"You could say that. I met the kid who did it. He's Chinese or Hmong or Tibetan or something. Maybe I'll write a piece on him, too—the mad scientist of Bloodwater High."

Her mother's eyes lit up. "He sounds interesting. A Tibetan chemist!"

Roni laughed. "I just meant he's Asian, Mom. Besides, he's a freshman, a geek, and he only comes up to my navel. Don't get your hopes up." She added, "Anyway, you wouldn't approve of him. He got suspended, too."

8

snatched

Brian felt as if a giant electromagnet were pulling him toward Bloodwater House.

He hadn't really planned on going there, but once he started walking, his feet just naturally pointed in that direction. It wasn't every day that somebody got abducted in Bloodwater. He had to know more, and the answers would be at the home of Alicia Camden and her younger brother, Ted Thorn.

If anybody could tell him more about the abduction, it would be Ted.

Brian knew Ted from science class. Ted was a year older than Brian, but he never lorded it over him. They had collaborated on a science fair project building a solar-powered potato gun. Brian had designed the gun. Ted had supplied the potatoes. The potato gun had worked great, but it had been confiscated when a slight miscalculation caused a large dent to appear on the fender of Principal Spindler's Buick.

Brian was about six blocks from Bloodwater House when a car pulled over to the curb next to him. It was Roni Delicata.

"Hey, Stink Bomb, where you headed?"

"Bloodwater House," said Brian.

"That's where I'm going. Hop in!"

Brian got into the car and Roni took off, wheels spinning.

"How come you're running around loose, Stink Bomb?" she asked. "Didn't your parents put you under house arrest?"

"My name's not Stink Bomb. It's Brian."

"Really? You don't *look* like a Brian."

"What's that supposed to mean?" Brian didn't like it when people made assumptions. She probably thought his name should be Chin, or Hop-Sing.

"I mean, you look like a Quincy. Or maybe a Hector, or a Zigmund. I expected you to have a really weird name, like a mad scientist. You being a mad stink bomber and all."

Oh. That was okay, then. The girl wasn't prejudiced—she was simply deranged.

Brian said, "I'll probably be grounded when my mom gets home, but my dad's clueless. How about you?"

"I'm going over to Alicia's to make the big apology. One way to get out of the house. Maybe she'll be cool and talk to me about what happened."

"I doubt it," Brian said.

"You don't have to be so negative."

"Well, I'm pretty sure about this. Alicia just got snatched."

9

alone

The boat cabin was smaller than the smallest closet in Bloodwater House. The only light came from two filthy portholes. Paint flaked from the walls and floor, and there were spiders everywhere. Alicia sat on the edge of a thin, rippled foam mattress. The cabin wasn't quite tall enough to stand up in, and it smelled of mold.

How long would it be before her mother knew she was missing?

Not long, Alicia thought. She would miss having someone she could order around. She would miss having someone to drag around on her stupid shopping safaris. She would miss having someone to show off to her friends: "Isn't she *adorable*? Why, she looks *just* like *I* did when *I* was her age, but she's *so* much more *athletic*! Alicia, dear, show Mrs. Wentworth your calves. Look at that. Aren't they so muscular? Can you imagine?"

Was there anybody in the entire universe as egocentric as her mother? She would probably assume that Alicia had walked home from the hospital, or gotten a ride from a friend.

She'd gotten a ride all right. And ended up stuck on this boat.

With a shudder, Alicia brushed a spider off her leg,

hugged her knees to her chest, and stared at the heavy wooden door.

She heard something scurry across the deck. A river rat, or something worse. Waves lapped against the sides of the boat, rocking it gently. Every now and then it would bump up against the dock and she would jump, thinking that she was hearing the thump of his heavy foot stepping onto the boat. She imagined the door opening . . .

What would happen to her?

10

the power of the press

"Snatched?" Roni said. "You mean abducted? When?"

"This afternoon, I suppose. I mean, you got in a fight with her at lunchtime, so it must've been after that."

"Where?"

"I don't know."

"How? Who? Why?"

"I don't know, I don't know, I don't know," Brian said.

Roni's heart was hammering. *Abducted!* The same person who had beaten Alicia in the park must have come back to kidnap her.

"I thought maybe Ted would know something," Brian said.

"Who's Ted?"

"Alicia's brother. He's kind of a friend of mine."

They rounded a curve and Bloodwater House came into view. Normally there was little traffic on Riverview Terrace, but today the road was lined with vehicles—two police cruisers and several other vehicles, including a bright yellow KDUK-TV van.

"You ever been inside?" Roni asked, looking up at the house.

"Just once. It's huge."

"No kidding." Bloodwater House was the biggest home in

Bloodwater, and one of the oldest. It had been built in the 1890s by James J. Bloodwater, the son of Zebulon J. Bloodwater, who had founded the town back in 1867. Built entirely of native limestone, Bloodwater House had four enormous pillars on either side of the front door. Roni had heard that there were more than thirty rooms inside. The house was completely surrounded by a ten-foot-tall wrought iron fence. Each vertical bar was topped by a large iron spear point.

Since James J. Bloodwater's death, the house had passed through a dozen owners. The house had a bad reputation. No one ever stayed for more than a few years. The latest in the long line of owners were Arnold and Alice Thorn, Alicia Camden's parents.

"Think they're gonna let us in?" Brian asked.

"Why not?" Roni said. "I'm here on official business. This is a big story."

Two policemen stood near the front gate talking to a woman with big blond hair and a microphone. Roni recognized her as Kerry Berry, the anchor for KDUK Channel 7 News. Several other reporter types were milling around, looking bored and frustrated.

The best strategy, Roni decided, was to just go for it. She pulled out her notebook and pen and walked up to the nearest policeman.

"Excuse me, I'm P. Q. Delicata, from the *Bloodwater Pump*. I wonder if you could answer some questions for me."

The cop looked down at her with an amused smile. "The

Bloodwater Pump? I remember that paper from high school. Sorry, we aren't supposed to talk to the press."

"You were talking to her." Roni pointed her pen at the blond news anchor.

Kerry Berry gave her a disdainful look. The cop shrugged. Roni decided to use an old reporter's trick she had read about. She said, "Is it true that Alicia Camden was kidnapped in broad daylight?"

The cop looked startled. "Where did you hear that?" he asked.

"I never reveal my sources," said Roni. She leaned in close to the cop and said in a low voice, "Yes or no? If you don't answer, I will take it as a yes."

The cop said, "Sorry, kid. Can't help you."

Roni frowned. Kerry Berry was looking at her with a smirk. Just then, through the gates, Roni saw Brian inside the fence standing beside a boy with thick blond hair. Brian saw her and waved, then pointed toward the gate at the back of the lot.

Roni looked at her watch and said to the cop, "I'd love to stay and chat, but I'm on deadline." She winked at Kerry Berry, then ran back along the iron fence.

11

three thorns

"She was waiting for our mom to pick her up in front of the hospital after her doctor appointment. Then somebody pulled up in an SUV, and Alicia got in, and they drove off. That was three hours ago. Nobody's seen her since." Ted Thorn offered this information unemotionally, as if he were giving an oral report at school.

Roni stared at Ted Thorn's head. Not a hair out of place. You would think that when your sister gets abducted, you would let your hair get a little mussed. They were in the backyard by the pentagonal swimming pool. Roni and Brian were sprawled in a couple of cedar deck chairs. Ted was standing at the edge of the pool with his hands in the pockets of his blue jeans. The jeans had a crisp crease down the front. Who irons blue jeans? Roni wondered.

"How come you and your sister have different last names?" she asked.

Ted looked uncomfortable. "When my mom married Arnold, we were all supposed to change our names to Thorn. Only Alicia kicked up a fuss, so they let her keep the name Camden, our real dad's name." He looked away. "Alicia doesn't care much for Arnold."

"Did anybody see who was driving the SUV?" Roni asked.

"I don't think so."

"Wait a sec—why do they think she was kidnapped?" Brian asked. "It sounds like she got into the car willingly. Maybe she's just riding around with a friend."

Ted shook his head. "Alicia doesn't really have any friends she hangs with. Except Maurice, and she broke up with him a few days ago. And she missed our French lesson. Our tutor comes here every Monday at three. She knows my mom would kill her if she missed French."

"Still," Roni said, "that doesn't mean she was *kidnapped*."

"I suppose. Except for what happened to her last Friday in the park. I think that's what's got everybody so freaked."

"So the police think the guy who grabbed her was the same guy that beat her up?"

"I don't know. My mom thinks it was our real dad. Only he lives halfway across the state in Mankato, and besides, he drives a pickup truck, not an SUV. He's a signpainter. Besides, he would never beat anybody up. Arnold thinks it's somebody who wants his money. Like a professional kidnapper."

"Have you seen any strangers hanging around?"

"Just that guy with the beard."

Roni asked quickly, "What guy is that?"

"That scruffy old guy, Driftwood Doug. You see him around. When we first moved here he came to our door and started yelling something about a curse. Arnold called the cops on him. I still see him cutting through our woods every now and then." Ted pointed past the swimming pool to the woods at the end of their yard. "Our property goes all the way down to the river."

"Driftwood Doug's been around for years," Roni said. "He's harmless."

"Did you tell the police about him?" Brian asked.

"Yeah. They seemed interested. Arnold told them he was the one that wrecked his boat."

"What boat?"

"Arnold had a boat." Ted pointed toward the river. "But it got vandalized, so he had to sell it."

"And you think Driftwood Doug wrecked the boat?"

Ted shrugged. "That's what Arnold told the cops."

Just then a tall, blond-haired man dressed in a suit walked out of the house. He moved like a dancer, and was smoking a cigarette. It had to be Arnold Thorn.

"Ted, you shouldn't be out here," said Arnold Thorn. "We don't want those newshounds spreading pictures of you all over the airwaves. One missing child is quite enough."

"Yes, sir."

Roni wasn't sure she had ever heard anyone call their father "sir" before. But what did she know—she didn't even have a father.

"And who are your friends?" Mr. Thorn asked, turning a forced smile on Roni and Brian.

"Just kids from school," Ted said. "I didn't invite them. They just stopped by."

"This isn't a good time for company, Ted."

"I know. I—"

"*There* you are!" Ted's mother came rushing out of the house. "I was worried about you, honey, I . . . who is this?"

"These are some friends of mine, Mom. This is Brian Bain, and this—"

"I know who *you* are." She pointed at Roni, and her neck turned instantly red while her face, covered with a thick layer of makeup, remained pale. "You're that awful girl who attacked Alicia!"

"I'm sorry," said Roni. "I'm really, really, really sorry about what happened this afternoon. I was just—"

"I don't care!" Mrs. Thorn said, advancing on Roni. "I want you out of here!"

"Okay, okay!" Roni stood up and started backing away.

"Mrs. Thorn? Is everything okay?" A small, dark-haired woman wearing a navy blue suit came out of the house. Roni noticed a police badge clipped to the woman's lapel.

"Detective, this *creature* is the girl who attacked my daughter this afternoon," said Mrs. Thorn. "Who knows, she might have something to do with what happened to Alicia!"

"Oh?" The policewoman peered closely at Roni, then asked, "Did you know Alicia well?"

"Not really," said Roni. "I'm writing a story for the school newspaper and—"

"I want her *out* of here," said Mrs. Thorn. "I want them *both* out of here!"

"Both?" the dark-haired woman asked, then did a double

take as she caught sight of Brian peeking out from behind Ted.

Her mouth fell open. "Brian? What on earth are you doing here?"

"Nothing, Mom," Brian sighed.

12

the plan

"I am so dead." Brian slumped down in his seat and stared gloomily out the windshield.

"You can't be dead," Roni said, making a U-turn on Riverview Terrace. "Your mouth is moving."

"I might as well be dead. My mom's gonna kill me."

"I doubt it. Mothers rarely kill their sons."

Brian looked at Roni. He was beginning to understand why Alicia had whacked her with a backpack.

"I wasn't being literal," he said.

"Okay then, I won't quote you." She winked.

Brian looked back at Bloodwater House. "Who do you think is scarier—Mr. or Mrs. Thorn?"

"Neither of them is as scary as your mom," said Roni.

Roni had been ordered to drive Brian home after his mother's quiet explosion outside the Bloodwater House. Amazing how his mother could do that—get really quiet and at the same time scare the liver out of you. She had told him, in no uncertain terms, to get his sorry butt home.

Roni said, "I'm just kidding. Your mom is a good connection."

"You wouldn't say that if you were connected to her," Brian said. "At least not when she's mad like that."

"She doesn't seem so bad. So . . . were you adopted or what?"

Brian was startled. It was obvious to anyone who had met his parents that he was adopted, but almost nobody came right out and asked.

"Why do you ask?" he asked.

"Because your mom doesn't look like you. What are you, Chinese? Vietnamese? Thai?"

"I'm American."

"I mean, where'd you come from originally?"

"From under a cabbage leaf."

"Okay, smart-ass."

To his own surprise, Brian didn't mind her calling him "smart-ass." The way she said it made it sound okay.

"Actually, I'm from South Korea," he said.

"Cool. South Korea. D'you like your parents?"

He shrugged. "They're okay, I guess."

"I know what you mean. I only have one. My mom, Nick."

"You call your mom Nick?"

"Yeah. I started doing it one day and she liked it. She's pretty cool. Except when she's on the warpath."

"Where's your dad?"

"Good question. All I got from him was my middle name."

"What is it?"

Roni didn't say anything for a couple of seconds, then

shrugged and said, "Quigley. Petronella Quigley Delicata. And if you ever tell anyone, I'll be forced to kill you. I am being literal."

"Your secret is safe with me."

"Good. So, will you help me?"

"Help you?"

"Yeah. Find out what your mom knows about Alicia's abduction."

"She doesn't like to talk about her work," Brian said.

"You just have to know how to ask the right questions."

When they reached Highway 61, Brian said, "My house is up that way." He pointed to the left.

Roni turned right.

"Hey, where are we going?" he asked.

"Look, Brian, we have a common agenda here. We're both kicked out of school and we're both grounded. Sometimes the best thing to do is lay low and be good for a while. But sometimes you just have to charge ahead, you know what I mean?"

"Not really."

"I think there's another way out of this mess. At least, for me. We conduct our own investigation."

"We?"

"You and me. You could be a big help."

Brian liked to be helpful. But this P. Q. Delicata was what his mother would describe as "nothing but trouble."

"You're saying that the best way to get out of a hole is to dig it deeper?" he asked.

Roni laughed. "Would you rather sit in the hole and pout?"

"No. But I don't see what we can do that the police aren't already doing."

"We can do a lot. We can learn everything the police know through your mom, plus we can find out our own information. Think about it. If we found Alicia we'd be heroes."

Suddenly Brian could see it. His mom beaming down at him. His father actually seeing him. All the kids at school tossing him up on their shoulders. Maybe even a park or a street named after him.

He took a closer look at the girl driving the car. She was hunched over the wheel, driving fast, her eyes bright with excitement. Did he want to get mixed up with some crazy girl reporter, middle name Quigley, chasing after dangerous kidnappers? Did he want to risk being grounded for all of eternity? Or did he want to go home and eat tuna melt sandwiches and listen to his father describe a new type of bovine pustule infestation?

He thought about it for three more seconds.

"What's the plan?" he asked.

13

leverage

"The plan is, first we find out who was driving the SUV that Alicia got into."

"Do you know how many SUVs there are in Bloodwater?"

"According to Ted, Alicia got into the car willingly. Maybe it was somebody she knew." Roni ticked off names on her fingers. "There's Alicia's real dad, then there's her step-dad, and her boyfriend, Maurice."

"Don't forget the guy who beat her up in the park," Brian said.

"I'm not forgetting that, but I don't know why she'd get into a car with a guy who had just beat her up."

"Maybe he was pointing a gun at her."

"Maybe. But let's start with Maurice."

"Okay." Brian thought for a second. "He's not home right now. He's at basketball practice."

"How do you know that?"

"I stay after school for Chess Club most Thursdays. Basketball practice lets out about the same time. I bet we could catch him in the parking lot in about twenty minutes."

"Twenty minutes, huh?" Because she hadn't eaten lunch Roni was suddenly very hungry. "A stop at the Dairy Queen might be in order."

Brian dug in his pocket. "I have enough for two Buster Bars."

Chocolate and white cotton don't mix, Roni thought as she rubbed with a paper napkin at the brown stain on her shirt. It wasn't doing much good—she was just spreading the chocolate over a larger area.

They were sitting in Roni's car in the school parking lot, waiting for the basketball players. The last bite of Roni's Buster Bar had missed her mouth and fallen onto her shirt. Roni gave it a few more halfhearted swipes, then gave up.

"You know what you'd do if you were smart?" Brian said.

Roni gave him a withering look.

"I don't mean you in particular," said Brian. "I mean everybody."

Roni said, "Okay, I'll bite. What would I do?"

"Wear clothes the same color as whatever you're going to eat."

"That's a pretty stupid idea."

"So's walking around with a big stain on your front."

"What if I wanted to eat a lime Popsicle? Green isn't my color. Or what if you wanted to eat strawberry ice cream. You think you'd look good in pink?"

"Sure, why not—hey, isn't that Maurice?"

A tall, broad-shouldered guy with short sandy hair, dark eyebrows, and the face of an angel was coming across the parking lot. A letter jacket was draped stylishly over one shoulder, and he walked with the bouncy step of a guy who looks good and knows it.

"That's him all right," Roni said. "Let's see which car is his."

Maurice stopped next to a red Camaro convertible. He shrugged into his letter jacket and took a key ring from his pocket. Roni's shoulders dropped in disappointment. Alicia had been seen getting into an SUV. A moment later her mouth fell open in astonishment when Maurice dragged a key from one end of the Camaro to the other, ripping a long, ugly scratch in the paint.

"Did you see that?"

Brian said, "Somebody's gonna be really irate."

"No kidding."

"Might give us a little leverage."

Roni looked over at Brian. "I like how you think."

Maurice, with a little smile on his angelic features, walked over to a green Ford Explorer SUV and opened the door.

"Bingo," said Roni.

14

king tut

"Maurice! Wait up!"

Maurice Wellington jumped as if he'd been goosed. He whirled and glared at Roni, who was trotting across the parking lot toward him.

"What?" said Maurice, scowling dangerously.

Brian followed Roni, staying a good ten feet back. He wasn't sure what she was going to do, and he didn't want to get too close. Athletic types could be touchy, and Maurice had a reputation for being extra prickly.

"Got a minute?" Roni asked.

"No," said Maurice, getting into his Explorer.

"I just have a couple of questions."

"About what?"

"Alicia Camden."

Maurice's mouth tightened. "What about her?"

"Do you know where she is?"

"No. I hope I never hear from her again."

"You're not worried?"

"Why should I be worried?"

"Because she was abducted."

He cocked his head. "Abducted? Really?"

"A couple of hours ago. By someone driving an SUV."

Roni pointed her pen at Maurice's Explorer. Brian thought that was a nice touch.

"Well, it wasn't me. Who are you, anyway?"

"Roni Delicata. I'm a reporter for the *Pump*."

Maurice made a face. "I don't talk to reporters."

"I'm different. You want to talk to me."

"Oh yeah?" Maurice's mouth curved into a nasty sneer. "And why is that?"

Roni matched his nasty sneer with a grin. "Because I just saw you key that Camaro."

As the blood drained out of Maurice's face, Brian thought, Now *that's* how to grill a suspect.

Just then, Brian saw a familiar figure come out of the school and walk around the corner toward the after-school buses. It was time to do a little interviewing of his own.

"If you want to know the truth . . . she dumped me," Maurice said. "She said I was too much like her stepdad."

Roni made a note in her ever-present notebook. "Are you?"

"Am I what?"

"Like her stepdad."

"No way. Have you met him? Mr. Thorn is totally full of himself. He wants everybody to think he's King Tut." Maurice crossed his arms and looked down at her, waiting for the next question.

"That's why you broke up? Because you're too much like Arnold Thorn?"

"I told you, I'm not like him at all."

Says you, Roni thought.

Maurice uncrossed his arms and buried his hands in the pockets of his letter jacket.

"Look," he said, "the real reason we broke up is because her mom thought I wasn't good enough for her. 'Cause I don't live in a mansion, I guess. Neither one of her parents liked me. Not that I care. Being Alicia's boyfriend was no picnic."

"Why was that?" Roni asked.

Maurice's mouth tightened. Roni thought he was going to shut down on her but then he spit it out. "There was no pleasing her. Like I couldn't possibly like her enough. I had to prove it all the time. I mean, every time we had an argument she expected me to bring her roses. You know how much roses cost?"

"Where were you at one o'clock this afternoon?"

"In school, where do you think?"

"Can you prove it?"

"Of course. There were only, like, thirty-five other kids in class."

She turned to ask Brian if he had any questions for Maurice, but Brian had disappeared.

"Now where did he go?" she wondered aloud.

"If you're talking about that goofy Asian kid, he took off. Look, I didn't kidnap Alicia, okay?"

"Any idea who did?"

"No. But it wouldn't surprise me if her real father came and got her. She told me he was really torn up about losing custody of her and her brother."

"The timing is just rather odd, after she got beat up and all."

"Well, it wasn't me." Maurice gave Roni a sideways look. "You aren't gonna tell Tyrone I keyed his car, are you?"

Roni looked back at the scratched Camaro. "Why do you have a problem with Tyrone?"

"I just do."

"Tell you what," she said. "If some anonymous benefactor pays Tyrone to have his car repainted, I won't say a word."

Maurice looked like he'd been kicked in the stomach. He made a sour face and said, "Okay. But if you're really serious about finding out what happened to Alicia, you should talk to *him*."

"Tyrone? Why?"

"Because he always had a thing for her. He was, like, obsessed."

15

prime suspect

Dante McQueen stuck up nearly a foot above all the other kids waiting for the after-school activities bus. Brian only came up to his elbow. Brian was more used to seeing him sitting—they played chess together whenever Dante could squeeze it in. Dante was a fierce competitor, and he loved chess more than anything.

But Dante's father had insisted that he try out for basketball. So while all his friends were working on their chess moves, Dante had to work on his layups.

"How was practice?" Brian asked.

"Pitiful. These guys don't even talk, they just grunt. Who won the chess tournament last week?"

"Beaner."

"He always wins." Dante sat down on the steps, his knees sticking up as high as his shoulders.

Brian stood in front of him, their eyes now on the same level. "Do you know Maurice Wellington very well?"

Dante shrugged. "As well as anybody."

"What happened with him and his girlfriend?"

"Alicia? I don't know. But he was sure shook up about it. You could see it in his playing. For the past couple of practices he's been kinda brain-dead, even for Maurice. And today he showed up late, which really pissed off Coach Brentwood. Said he had a dentist appointment."

"He left school early this afternoon?"

"Yeah, he left at lunchtime." Dante stood up. "My bus is here."

Brian scrambled, trying to think like Roni, trying to come up with more questions. Only one occurred to him. "On a scale of one to ten, ten being pure monster, one being a mouse, how dangerous would you say Maurice is?"

Dante didn't even think about it. "Nine."

Brian was startled. "Nine?"

"Let me put it this way," Dante said. "Maurice doesn't care about anybody but Maurice, and he'll do anything he thinks he can get away with to get what he wants." He stepped onto the bus, then turned back to Brian and said, "If I were you, I'd stay out of his way."

"Thanks," Brian said. He headed back to the parking lot. Maybe he shouldn't have left Roni alone with Maurice. It sounded as if he was capable of anything. Kidnapping, for example. Brian started running. Even more than being afraid for Roni, he was excited to tell her what he'd learned. But when he reached the parking lot, Roni's car was there, but Roni was gone.

And so was Maurice's SUV.

16

left, right, left

Roni found Tyrone Eakin in the gym shooting baskets all by himself. She watched him shooting free throw after free throw. He was sinking only about one out of three. Roni was no basketball expert, but this guy definitely needed the practice.

After missing six in a row, Tyrone noticed Roni watching him.

"Hey," he said. His mahogany skin glistened with sweat. He turned back to the basket and sent the ball sailing in a nearly perfect arc. Not perfect enough. It hit the back of the rim and bounced off. Tyrone grabbed the ball and looked at Roni again. "I'm having an off day," he said.

"Me, too," said Roni.

"Yeah? What's your problem?"

"I got suspended. You're Tyrone Eakin, right?"

"Uh-huh." He started bouncing the ball: *left hand, right hand, left hand, right hand*. "How do you know that?"

Roni smiled. Everybody knew who Tyrone Eakin was. In addition to being close to six and a half feet tall, he was one of only a half dozen African American students at Bloodwater High. "I'm a basketball fan," she said.

"That so." He gave her a cautious smile. *Left hand, right hand, left hand . . .*

"You know Alicia Camden, right?"

"Uh-huh." The bouncing sped up a little. *Left, right, left, right.*

"I suppose you heard what happened a few hours ago."

"Nope. What happened?" *Left, right, left . . .*

"Alicia was abducted."

The bouncing stopped.

"Seriously?"

"Yes. She was seriously abducted."

"By who?"

"I don't know. Do you?"

"Me? I don't even know her that well."

"I thought you were obsessed with her."

"Where'd you hear that?"

"From Maurice."

Tyrone laughed and started bouncing his ball again. *Left right left right.* "Alicia, she's too skinny for me."

Roni liked the idea of Alicia being too skinny. "Then why does Maurice think you have a thing for her?"

"I just talk to her sometimes is all. Just to mess with Maurice's head. Keep him on his toes, you know? He gets kind of full of himself sometimes."

"I heard she dumped him."

"That's what I heard, too."

"And you decided to move in?"

Left right left right. "Move in? Nah, I told you, girl. Not my type."

"Any idea who beat her up? Or might have wanted to kidnap her?"

"Nope." *Left right left right left right left* . . .

The bouncing was really getting on Roni's nerves, so she said the one thing she knew would stop it.

"Thanks, Tyrone. By the way, I was just out in the parking lot . . . what the heck happened to the side of your car?"

Brian had never liked waiting.

He was sitting on the hood of Roni's car. He wished she hadn't locked it. This waiting wouldn't be so bad if he could sit inside and listen to the radio. He figured he'd give Roni sixty seconds to show up. If she didn't, he'd call his mom.

Sixty seconds passed. No Roni. Okay, another sixty seconds.

Was Maurice really as dangerous and crazy as Dante claimed? And if he was crazy enough to kidnap his ex-girlfriend, did that mean he was crazy enough to snatch Roni, too? And even if he'd wanted to, could he? Brian tried to imagine forcing Roni into a car. She'd be like a wild cat. Even a big guy like Maurice would have a tough time of it.

Where *was* she?

If he called his mom, he'd have to explain to her why he was sitting in the school parking lot when she'd ordered him to go straight home. Maybe he would call 911. An anonymous call. Tell them they had another possible abduction.

Another sixty seconds passed.

He tried to think of where the nearest phone might be. Inside the school? He really didn't want to go back inside the school. If Spindler caught him he'd be toast for sure. On the other hand, if Maurice had abducted Roni . . .

Brian heard the sound of size 13 basketball shoes slapping asphalt. He looked up to see Tyrone Eakin charging across the parking lot. Tyrone ran up to the red Camaro, saw the scratch Maurice had made, and let out a howl of rage.

"Told you somebody was gonna be irate," Brian muttered to himself. Looking back at the school, he saw Roni trotting toward him, a little smile on her face.

"Where did *you* disappear to?" Brian asked as she got closer.

"Me?" Roni unlocked her car. "You're the one who went running off."

Tyrone was staring goggle-eyed at the scratch on his car, dancing from foot to foot, ranting in language foul enough to melt paint.

Brian said, "We better get the bleeping bleep out of here."

"Watch your bleeping language, Stink Bomb," Roni said.

17

the collector

"One more stop," Roni said as they drove off, leaving Tyrone and his temper tantrum in the school parking lot.

Brian looked at his watch. "I should get home pretty soon."

"This won't take long," Roni said. "Probably."

Brian didn't like the sound of that. "Look, if I'm not home when my mom gets there, I'm dog meat."

"I don't think you get it, Stink Bomb. This isn't a game. This is for real. Someone snatched Alicia." Roni honked the horn for no good reason. "She could be dead."

"And you think *we're* going to save her?"

"Why not?" She pulled onto the highway leading south out of town.

"Do you think it was Maurice?" Brian asked.

"No. He was in class all afternoon."

"Why do you think that?"

"Because he told me." Roni looked at Brian. "It would be so easy to check I figure he wouldn't lie about it. Why?"

"Because Dante McQueen told me that Maurice left school at lunchtime."

Roni took her foot off the gas. "And you're telling me this now?"

"You think I should have waited longer?"

Roni shook her head. "I guess Maurice is back on the list of suspects." She gave Brian a sideways look. "Listen, if we're going to work together, we've got to learn to communicate."

"Okay. Are you going to communicate to me where we're going?"

"We're going to pay a visit to Driftwood Doug."

"Oh." Brian felt his heart jump in his chest. "But doesn't he live on—"

Roni finished his sentence for him. "—Wolf Spider Island."

Wolf Spider Island was infamous for its ramshackle collection of bobbing constructions that were not quite houses, not quite boats, and not quite legal. There were two- and three-story houseboats, floating geodesic domes, and even the back half of a school bus mounted on oil-barrel pontoons. Many of these floating residences were painted in bright, garish colors, with each resident seeking to outdo his neighbor.

The residents of Wolf Spider Island were no less bizarre than their homes. Roni had once written an article for the *Pump* about the loosely knit group of aging hippies, bikers, artists, and fishermen who populated the floating city.

Last summer the mayor, Buddy Berglund, had gotten all worked up about the island.

"Criminals, perverts, and weirdos," he had said, slamming his pudgy fist on his desk. Roni's mother had to calm him down, as she often did. The reason he was upset, it turned out, was because his daughter was dating a scraggly, moccasin-wearing, non-tax-paying candlemaker who lived in a tent on the island. Fortunately, the daughter broke up with the candlemaker before Buddy could nuke the island.

What Roni liked about Wolf Spider Island was the sense of a classic "place that time forgot." Still, it could be a scary place. For one thing, there really *were* wolf spiders on the island, and they were huge. And even though most of the islanders were nice people, there were definitely a few weirdos in the mix.

Driftwood Doug was one of the island's best-known residents. Every now and then Roni would see him tramping through the woodlands, wading through the marshes, and exploring the riverbanks in his canoe. He always wore the same red-checked flannel shirt, the same blue denim bib overalls, the same clunky boots and scraggly reddish-brown beard, the same canvas tote bag over one shoulder. He always seemed to be collecting something—driftwood, mushrooms, wild plums, aluminum cans—anything he could sell.

Roni now wondered if Driftwood Doug might have collected himself a teenage girl.

18

devil face

Roni turned off the highway south of town onto a narrow track that led across a field and into the woods along the edge of the river. She stopped the car in the unofficial parking lot for the island, a deserted, grassy clearing at the edge of the woods. The other vehicles parked there included an SUV, a couple of motorcycles, and an old Volkswagen van spray painted with Day-Glo daisies and peace signs.

Brian looked at her. "I've never been here before."

"Don't worry. There aren't actually that many wolf spiders," Roni said.

"You hang out here a lot?"

"I've been here a couple of times."

She got out of the car, but Brian didn't.

"You really think Driftwood Doug has something to do with Alicia being missing?" Brian asked.

"Who knows? We know he was lurking around Bloodwater House. Maybe he kidnapped Alicia for ransom. Or maybe he's deranged."

"Deranged? Great. By all means, let's go see him."

"Come on, Stink Bomb. What could possibly happen?"

"We could get abducted and thrown in a pit." Brian looked at Roni with a deadpan expression. "Technically, one could say that you have abducted me." He looked at his watch. "And if I'm not home in about forty-five minutes, my mom's gonna kill me."

She looked at him, sitting in her car with no expression on his face. A laugh burbled up inside her and she snorted. "Okay, forty-five minutes. This won't take that long."

With a reluctant shrug, Brian got out of the car and followed her down a dirt path and over a rickety wooden bridge that crossed the channel to the island. A narrow path snaked through a dense woods of cottonwood, willow, and river birch. They followed the trail to a path that branched off toward the shore.

"This way," said Roni, acting more confident than she felt. The path led to a rickety wooden dock that jutted out into the river.

A boy about Brian's age was fishing off the end of the dock.

"Catching anything?" Roni asked.

"Not yet," the boy said, keeping his eyes on his bobber.

"You know which boat belongs to Driftwood Doug?" Roni asked.

The boy pointed to a gap in the trees. "You take that path till you get to a tree with a face carved in it. If this big brown dog comes charging at you, just yell at him real loud and he'll leave you alone. Hang a right at the face, then follow the shoreline till you get to Driftwood Doug's. You'll know which one it is when you get there. Only he ain't home right now. I saw him heading upriver in his canoe about half an hour ago."

"Was he alone?"

"Driftwood Doug is always alone."

Branches and tall weeds brushed against them on either side as they followed the narrow path. Roni imagined wolf spiders, poison ivy, and large brown dogs.

"I'm glad this was your idea," Brian said as they pushed through a patch of stinging nettles. "I'd hate to have thunk it up myself."

After a few minutes the path widened and the underbrush thinned out. They could see the river again. They passed a houseboat that looked like a gingerbread house, and another that was nothing more than a ragged nylon tent sitting on a floating plywood platform.

"There's the face," said Brian, pointing at a gnarly old cottonwood. A scowling devil face four feet tall had been carved into the trunk. They heard a dog barking, but it sounded as if it was a long way off. They followed a well-worn track toward the shore until they came to a pile of driftwood ten feet tall. "I'd say this is the place," he said.

On the other side of the woodpile was a fire pit with a grate, a few rusted metal lawn chairs, and a two-story houseboat that seemed to be tilted toward the river. The front ends of the pontoons were riding up on shore.

"Anybody home?" she yelled.

Nobody answered.

She turned and looked at Brian. Brian looked at his

watch. She felt like ripping it off his wrist and throwing it in the river.

"If you want, you can go back to the car," she snapped.

"No way. If I go back to the car, you'll be out here for hours."

"Okay then." Roni returned her attention to the houseboat. "Let's check it out." She stepped onto the pontoon and pulled herself up over the railing.

19

the bloodwater connection

Brian watched Roni edge along the narrow, tilting deck, peering into the cabin through the two porthole windows. He added breaking and entering to the list of crimes he could be charged with, then hopped up onto the boat to join her.

"I can't see anything from out here," Roni said.

"Maybe we should try knocking."

"I'm pretty sure there's nobody in there."

The door was at the back of the boat. Roni rapped on it a few times, listened, then twisted the doorknob.

The door swung open.

"Hello?" Roni said. "Anybody home?"

"What do you see?" Brian asked.

Roni stepped into the dark interior.

"Wow," she said.

Brian blinked as he peered through the door into the cabin of the boat. His eyes adjusted to the dim light, and he saw a long wooden table piled with twisted, light brown . . . somethings.

"What are they?" he said.

"I don't know," Roni said. "They look like some kind of roots." She picked one up. It looked like a carrot gone insane, with the main root splitting into two rootlets like a pair of twisted, tapering legs.

"You think he eats them?"

Roni sniffed the root and made a face. "Smells like old wood."

They looked around at the rest of the room. There were two beat-up wooden chairs, a large plastic cooler, and a long bookshelf made from scrap lumber. The shelves were crammed with books. Brian read a few of the titles: *Mushrooms of North America*, *The Adventures of Huckleberry Finn*, *The Survivalist's Bible*, *The Nick Adams Stories* . . .

"I guess he likes to read," Brian said.

"Good one, Brainiac," said Roni. She was climbing a ladder up to the second level. "Check this out," she said.

Brian didn't want to follow her. But he didn't want to be left behind, so he grabbed onto the ladder and climbed up after her.

Like the main floor, the loft was sparsely furnished: a thin mattress neatly dressed with sheets and a blanket, another well-stocked bookshelf, a small desk and chair, and an old trunk. Light slanted in through a skylight.

At one end of the room hung several pairs of denim bib overalls and the same number of red-checked flannel shirts.

"You notice anything weird?" Roni asked.

Brian glanced around the small loft. "You notice anything *not* weird?"

"It's so . . . *organized*."

"Yeah. The guy lives in a tilted houseboat but there isn't a speck of dust anywhere."

"And check out the wardrobe. He only wears one outfit, but he's got a ten-day supply."

"But no Alicia."

"I guess not. If he took her he must have stashed her someplace else." Roni noticed a framed photograph on top of the dresser.

"You think this is him in the picture?" Roni asked. The photo showed a smiling, clean-cut man and a pretty, dark-haired woman standing in front of a building.

"I don't know."

Roni picked up the photo and held it up to the skylight. "In the background . . . isn't that Bloodwater House?"

Brian took a closer look. He could make out the large stone walls and windows. "It sure looks like it." He turned the frame over and looked at the back. "Uh-oh."

Taped to the back of the frame was a picture cut from a newspaper. It showed a man, a woman, and two teens smiling into the camera.

"Recognize anybody?" Brian asked.

"The Thorns!" Roni said. "That was the picture that was in the paper when they first bought Bloodwater House!"

Suddenly the boat rocked and Brian felt his heart thump. He hoped it was just a wave.

Roni put the photo back on the dresser. "Maybe we should go," she whispered.

"I'm with you," Brian said. He was already scooting down the ladder. He wanted to get off that boat as quickly as possible. He practically ran across the cabin, not waiting for Roni. He wanted to get out of there. He had a bad feeling.

Brian burst through the door and was just stepping out onto the deck when an arm the size of a tree limb wrapped around his waist and lifted him into the air.

20

hoot

"Hey!" Brian shouted, instinctively flailing his arms and kicking at his attacker.

The man shifted his grip, grabbing Brian's belt and dangling him over the water. Brian stopped struggling. He did not want to get dropped into the river. It looked wet.

"Got me a little river rat." The voice sounded like a gravel truck emptying its load.

Brian twisted his head to look at his captor. He did not like what he saw.

The man's head was completely hairless and as shapeless as a lump of raw dough. Worst of all, he was grinning. The grin could have used about six more teeth.

"What you doin', li'l riv rat?" the man rumbled.

"Let me down and I'll tell you," Brian said.

The man laughed. It was not a pretty sound. His whole body, all three hundred pounds of it, shook when he laughed. Brian hoped his belt wouldn't snap.

"Hey, Hoot," said Roni.

"Who's that?" the man rumbled, looking back at Roni. "I know you?"

"It's me, Hoot. Roni Delicata. Remember me?"

"Oh yeah," said Hoot. "The reporter girl."

"That's right. How about you put my friend down?"

"This little rat's with you?"

"Yes."

"Huh! You a burglar now?"

"We just came out here to talk to Driftwood Doug. The door was open, so we went in."

"Good thing I happened by. Just checkin' on Doug's boat on account of we got a big storm rollin' in. Just in time to keep you from making off with all his worldly possessions."

"We didn't take anything."

" 'Cuz Hootie come along to stop ya."

"No, because we aren't thieves."

"You sure?"

"Of course I'm sure! Why don't you put him down, Hoot, and I'll introduce you."

Hoot looked back at Brian as if he had forgotten about him, then brought him back over the boat and set him down gently.

Brian looked up at the man mountain from his new perspective. Next to Roni, he looked like a giant troll dressed in jeans and a black leather vest.

Roni said, "Hoot, this is my friend Brian. Brian, this is Hoot."

"Please to mee'cha," said Hoot. He grabbed Brian's hand and pumped it so hard Brian thought his shoulder would dislocate. Hoot released Brian's hand and returned his attention to Roni. "How come you two burglin' Doug's boat?"

"I told you," Roni said. "We didn't take anything. We just wanted to talk to him."

"Shouldn't go on people's boats without an invite."

"I know. I'm sorry, Hoot."

"Sorry don't cut it, girl. Down here on the island we got to take care of each other."

Roni said, "Hoot, we really don't have time to talk. I have to be getting home, okay?"

"You kids comin' down here causin' all kinds a trouble." Hoot crossed his arms over his massive chest. "People livin' on the island you be better off not knowin'."

Yeah, Brian thought, like you.

"We'll keep that in mind, Hoot," said Roni. "Next time."

"Ain't gonna be no next time."

"Listen, we have to go now, Hoot."

He shook his head. "Uh-uh, little girl. I think maybe I gonna turn you two over to the gestapo." Hoot glared at them from beneath his hairless brow, and Brian found himself wishing that he had just dropped him in the river.

love or money

"It's almost six," Brian said as he buckled his seat belt. It was a good habit, especially with Roni behind the wheel. "My mom's gonna lock me in my room for a year."

"Sorry," said Roni. She pulled onto the highway and headed for Bloodwater. "I didn't expect us to get busted."

"So . . . who *was* that guy?" Brian asked.

"That was the mayor of Wolf Spider Island."

They hadn't had a chance to talk during the walk back to the parking area with Hoot lumbering along behind them muttering about what he was going to do the next time he caught them "snoopin' and burglin'."

"They have their own *mayor*?"

"Unofficial mayor." Roni smiled. She had met Hoot back when she'd written the article on Wolf Spider Island. He wasn't as tough as he looked. Or maybe he was, but he had a soft heart. She was surprised how long it had taken her to talk him into letting her and Brian go. "He sort of keeps an eye on things."

"What was he talking about, turning us over to the gestapo?"

"That's what he calls the police. The Wolf Spider Islanders don't like cops. He wasn't really going to turn us in. Too much trouble. Basically, Hoot is pretty lazy."

Several huge raindrops splashed the windshield. Lightning flickered on the horizon. They rode in silence for a few minutes. The rain began to fall steadily.

"I guess we didn't find out much," Roni said as she turned onto Brian's street.

Roni stopped the car in front of Brian's house. The rain was coming down harder, and every few strokes of the windshield wipers brought another rumble of thunder.

Brian said, "We didn't find Alicia. But we know from that photo that Driftwood Doug has some connection with Bloodwater House."

"That doesn't mean he snatched Alicia."

"Maybe not," Brian said. "But it must mean *something*."

Brian was pretty sure he had beat his mother home, but he knew enough not to come sauntering in the front door. Just on the off chance she was sitting in the kitchen, he circled their split-level house and entered through the basement door. He could claim he had been home all the time. She might believe him.

He entered quietly and stopped at the bottom of the stairs. He didn't hear any conversation. More importantly he didn't hear the radio or the TV. His mother was a news addict. She had to know what was going on in the world all the time.

Brian walked up the stairs that ended in the kitchen. His father was hunched over the kitchen counter. A loaf of bread and a can of tuna sat at the end of the counter. In front of his father were four piles of cards. His father was playing bridge.

Most people played bridge with other people, but his father had devised a way that he could play it with himself. When Brian had asked him why he didn't play with other people, his dad told him it was just too much trouble. He could play for hours.

"Hey, Dad," Brian said.

His father lifted his head and smiled as if he had just woken up from a pleasant dream. "Brian, where have you been?"

"Around."

"I see. I thought maybe you'd left. Are you hungry, son?"

Brian liked it when his dad called him son. "Is Mom coming home for dinner or not?"

"She called again. She thought she'd swing by and eat with us, but then she's going to have to go back to work tonight."

Brian looked at the bread and tuna on the counter. "Tuna melts?"

"Yes. Just let me finish this hand. . . ."

Brian took over the sandwich-making process. He made the tuna salad with lots of finely chopped dill pickles. He lined up three pieces of bread on a cookie sheet, slathered on the tuna salad, and completely covered that with thinly sliced cheese.

"Dad, why would someone abduct a teenage girl?"

"I won," his father declared and slid all the cards back together. "Abduct a girl? Oh yes, your classmate."

"Yeah. What would be their motive?"

69

His father took only a moment to think and then he said, "Well, it could be for money, of course. Kidnapping for ransom is not unknown. There are also a number of mental aberrations that might lead to such antisocial behaviors. Early childhood trauma, brain tumor, social marginalization caused by political or cultural pressures, certain chemical imbalances in the brain leading to . . ."

Brian was often impressed by his father's ability to take a simple question and make it incredibly complicated. He decided to interrupt.

"But what is the most likely reason?"

Bruce Bain stopped talking and thought for a moment. "I believe that most child abductions occur when a parent abducts his or her own child."

"But why?"

"Often it is a couple who divorce, and the court gives custody to one parent, and then the other parent abducts the child. It must be terrible for the child."

"Do you think Alicia Camden's real father might have kidnapped her?"

"Without more facts, I would not care to speculate."

"What about being kidnapped by an ex-boyfriend? Does that ever happen?"

"Where human relations are concerned, particularly jealousy, almost anything is possible."

The front door banged open and his mother walked in the door shaking water off her umbrella.

"Hullo, dear," said Mr. Bain. "Is it raining out?"

"No," said Mrs. Bain. "It's pouring."

Brian turned on the grill and put the sandwiches under the broiler. When he turned back, his mother was smiling at him.

"You made dinner?" she asked.

"No big deal."

She messed up his hair and kissed him on the cheek. "Mom!" he protested—but actually he was glad she wasn't still mad at him.

"You're a good kid," she said. "Give me a second to wash up and put on a different pair of shoes. These things are killing me."

When they all sat down at the kitchen counter with the tuna melts perfectly melted, Brian brought up the topic of Alicia's abduction. "Have you found out anything?"

"We have some ideas, but we haven't yet located Alicia," she said, taking a careful bite of her tuna melt. She could never wait until it had cooled off. "Hot," she mumbled, waving her hand in front of her mouth.

"Do you have any ideas about the motive?"

"Well, keep in mind that we aren't absolutely certain she has been abducted. She may have gone with someone willingly. We are considering every possibility."

"But suppose she *was* abducted. Why would someone do that?"

"That's easy," said Mrs. Bain. "It usually comes down to love, money, or revenge. By the way, what on earth were you doing at the Thorns' today?"

"Ted's a friend of mine. We did that science project together, remember?"

"Oh yes . . . the potato gun."

"Dad says that most kidnappings are parents snatching their own kids."

"That's true, but that usually involves younger children. Why? Did Ted say something about his father?"

"You mean Mr. Thorn?"

"No, his real father." His mother caught herself. "I mean his biological father."

"He mentioned him. He lives in Mankato. They hardly ever see him. Is he a suspect?"

"The Mankato police have been trying to locate him."

"He's missing, too?"

"According to his neighbor, he left on a fishing trip. I'm sure he'll turn up."

"So why do you think he did it? Love, money, or revenge?"

"I didn't say he did anything. We just want to talk to him." Mrs. Bain took another bite of her sandwich and chewed, giving Brian a suspicious look. After she had swallowed she said, "Why so many questions? Are you up to something, Brian?"

"No! Nothing!"

"I see," she said dryly. "How unusual."

22

river dance

Alicia felt like throwing up. Was it possible to get seasick on a river? Another gust of wind sent the boat rocking. She imagined the boat tearing loose from its moorings and traveling down the Mississippi River, all the way to New Orleans. She'd always wanted to go there. She imagined herself floating gently through the Mississippi bayous listening to the sound of Cajun music.

When she was in a tough spot, Alicia could always get away. For as long as she could remember, she had been able to escape to fantasies in her imagination. Maybe that's how she had survived the last few months without going completely crazy.

A wave slammed against the side of the boat, reminding her where she was.

It was getting dark outside. She hadn't eaten in hours, not since she'd finished her Snickers bar. She tried to persuade herself that might be good. She was always trying to lose weight. Still, her stomach felt like there was a small rat gnawing away at the inside of it.

She couldn't think about that. Hunger was the least of her problems. Instead, she imagined herself at the homecoming dance. She saw herself spinning across the dance floor in the perfect dress, black, spaghetti straps, fitting her to a T.

A huge gust of wind grabbed at the boat, tipping it almost on its side. She heard the sharp snap of a rope breaking, and then another, and suddenly the boat was spinning and rocking crazily, and the dress flew from her thoughts, and the dance floor vanished.

23

the curse

Roni stared at the big bloody brick squatting in the middle of the table.

"It's about time you showed up," Nick said. "Sit down. We're ready to eat."

Roni took her seat at the kitchen table, looking warily at what she feared was her dinner. Nick sat down across from her and used a bread knife to cut a thick slice of the catsup-topped meat loaf.

"You were gone a long time," Nick said. "You must have gotten on well with Alicia."

One of the things that amazed Roni about her mother was her eternal optimism. She always thought the best of people. In many ways, this worked to her mother's advantage—people often behaved better than usual because she expected them to.

"Actually, I never saw her," she said as her mother deposited a thick slab of gray matter onto Roni's plate.

"Oh? What have you been doing?"

"When I got to Alicia's there were cops all over the place, but no Alicia." Roni paused, letting the suspense build for a couple of seconds. "They think maybe she got abducted."

"Abducted?" Nick dropped the slice of meat loaf she was

moving toward her own plate. It hit the table with a thud. "Are you serious?"

"Yeah. Some guy grabbed her while she was waiting outside the hospital. Her mom's freaking."

"I imagine she is! A kidnapping in Bloodwater!" She shook her head and made a second attempt to load the slice of meat loaf onto her plate. "The mayor will be apoplectic."

Roni stuck her fork into the meat loaf and sawed off a chunk with her knife.

"Mom, is this one of your *special* recipes?"

"It's low fat, dear. I made it with extra-lean organic beef, soy flour, fat-free yogurt, and bulgur wheat. Remember, you said you wanted to lose a few pounds."

Roni sampled a small piece. Half a minute later she was still chewing. How tragic that a cow had died to make something so inedible.

"Interesting texture," she mumbled. She would definitely lose weight trying to eat this concoction. She could feel the calories burning off as she tried to chew a second piece.

"How awful!" Nick said.

At first Roni thought that her mother meant the meat loaf, but Nick was back on the subject of Alicia.

"That poor family has been under so much stress lately. And now this!"

Sometimes it seemed as if her mother knew every single person in this town of thirty thousand people—not only knew them, but knew who they were related to and who they knew and how they knew who they knew.

"What kind of stress?" Roni asked.

"That house, Bloodwater House . . . Arnold Thorn had such good intentions. He wanted to turn it into a showcase. He took out building permits for some major renovations, but they just haven't been able to find the financing."

"I thought they were rich."

"Not rich enough, apparently. That old house is a money pit."

Roni thought of the photo they had seen on Driftwood Doug's boat. "Who owned Bloodwater House before the Thorns?"

"Oh, it's gone through many, many owners. No one stays for long. That house has been nothing but trouble for everyone who has owned it. Let's see . . . when I first started working for the mayor it was owned by a man named Campbell. He had it for less than a year and then he disappeared. Ran away from some gambling debts, I heard. No one has heard from him since. The bank took over the property and sold it to Douglas and Cecilia Unger, a nice young couple. That house bankrupted them, and poor Cecilia committed suicide. She hanged herself to death from that awful iron fence."

"What happened to the husband?"

"Obviously he couldn't live there anymore. He simply walked away from it, and the bank took over the property again. It sat vacant for years before Arnold Thorn came along and bought it."

Nick took a bite of meat loaf, chewed on it for a while, and swallowed. Roni watched the lump work its way slowly down her mother's throat.

"It's a little chewy," Nick said.

"It doesn't actually *taste* all that bad," Roni offered.

Nick pushed her plate away. "How do you feel about ordering a pizza?"

After the two of them had put away an entire pepperoni and green olive pizza, Roni helped Nick clean the kitchen. The meat loaf went straight into the trash.

"Maybe next time I'll skip the soy flour," Nick said.

"How about next time we skip straight to the pizza," Roni suggested.

Nick laughed.

One thing about her mom, Roni thought. She had a sense of humor.

When they were done cleaning up, Roni went up to her room and turned on her laptop. Technically, under the terms of her punishment, she was supposed to use her computer for homework only. But *technically,* she had once read, bumblebees should not be able to fly. She signed on and opened up her mail program. Only one message.

From: BB2@brucebainbooks.net
To: PQDelicata@cityofbloodwater.gov
Subject: Alicia

Hey Roni, is that you?
Brian

78

Roni smiled at the e-mail message on her laptop. How had he found her e-mail address? She burped pepperoni and green olive pizza and typed in a reply.

From: PQDelicata@cityofbloodwater.gov
To: BB2@brucebainbooks.net
Subject: Re: Alicia

How'd you find me?
Roni

The reply came back almost immediately.

From: BB2@brucebainbooks.net
To: PQDelicata@cityofbloodwater.gov
Subject: Re: Alicia

I hacked everybody's e-mail addresses from the
school computer. ;-)
Have you looked outside? It's raining cats and
elephants out there. BTW I found out some stuff
from my mom. Guess who's the #1 suspect.
B

From: PQDelicata@cityofbloodwater.gov
To: BB2@brucebainbooks.net
Subject: Re: Alicia

Douglas Unger?
Roni

From: BB2@brucebainbooks.net
To: PQDelicata@cityofbloodwater.gov
Subject: Re: Alicia

Actually, it's Alicia and Ted's real dad. My mom
says they're trying to track him down, but
nobody knows where he is.
BTW, who's Douglas Unger?
B

From: PQDelicata@cityofbloodwater.gov
To: BB2@brucebainbooks.net
Subject: Re: Alicia

We have to talk. Can you—uh-oh, POS

Roni hit the send button and turned to face her mother,
the Parent Over Shoulder.

"What are you working on?" Nick asked.

"A story for the paper." It was only half a lie, Roni rea-
soned. If she could figure out what had happened to Alicia it
would make one heck of a story. "That's okay, isn't it?"

Roni knew her mother was proud of her for writing for
the school newspaper. Nick's dream was that Roni might one
day become the editor of the *Bloodwater Clarion*. But Roni
had bigger plans—like being an investigative reporter for
the *Washington Post*.

"Yes, of course, but shouldn't you turn your computer off
during a thunderstorm?"

"Yes, but—"

A blinding flash of lightning was followed instantly by a huge clap of thunder. The lights went out. Roni's computer stuttered, emitted a piteous beep, then the screen went to black.

24

overboard

How long had she been adrift? An hour? Two hours?

Alicia stood on the deck in the driving rain, wet hair plastered to her skull. It was coming down so hard she couldn't see either shore. A flash of lightning revealed the broken door to the cabin. It had been easy to kick the door open, once she had set her mind to it. But what good had it done her? She was stuck on a runaway boat with no way to control it.

She couldn't start the engine—he had taken the key.

She should go back inside, get out of the rain, and wait for the boat to wash up on shore. But where would that be? She might float for miles, maybe even as far as the lock and dam at Alma. And then what? With the storm filling the river past its banks, she might be swept over the dam to her death.

Alicia sometimes thought she would be better off dead. But she did not want to die.

Another flash of lightning lit up the choppy, rain-spattered surface of the river. Dead ahead floated an enormous tree that had been torn up by its roots. Alicia had no time to brace herself. The front of the boat rode up onto the floating trunk and the deck suddenly tilted. Alicia's feet went out from under her. She caught the gunwale as she went over the side and for a moment she hung there, her legs trailing in the cold river water, but the boat spun against the tree and a branch swept her off like a giant broom. Alicia grabbed for the branch, but caught only a handful of leaves that tore away as her head slipped beneath the muddy, storm-battered surface of the Mississippi.

25

style

Roni's mother spent most of the next morning at home fielding phone calls. Every time she hung up the phone and tried to leave for city hall, the phone would ring again. Alicia Camden's disappearance had hit the news, and the mayor, Buddy Berglund, was being bombarded with calls from reporters. Buddy, as usual, simply forwarded all his calls to Nick.

To make matters worse, last night's storm had knocked over dozens of trees and electric lines. They hadn't gotten their power back at home until almost six in the morning.

Roni stayed in her room reading stupid magazines and mourning her deceased laptop. She felt completely cut off from the world outside her bedroom. At one point she got so bored she decided to look in the mirror and give herself a pep talk.

"Hey, it's just for a day or two, then Nick will forget she grounded you."

"Nick never forgets anything."

"She'll get tired of you moping around the house. By the way, you could stand to lose a few pounds."

"My weight is normal for my height."

"Yeah, but you'd look a lot better if you were ten pounds lighter."

"I'm not obsessed with my appearance."

"Then why are you looking in this mirror?"

Oh well, so much for the pep talk.

Nick finally left at eleven. As soon as she drove off, the phone started jangling again. Roni ignored the ringing, laced up her good walking boots, threw on her pea green trenchcoat and a pair of sunglasses, and headed for Brian's house.

"I spent all morning trying to get hold of you," Brian said. "All I got was meep-meep-meep on the phone, and you never answered my e-mails."

"It's been kind of a zoo," Roni said. "We lost our power last night, my computer got fried, and Nick was on the phone all morning doing damage control. Alicia's disappearance has hit the news big-time."

"I know. My mom got about fifty phone calls last night, too. So who is this Douglas Unger?"

"Douglas Unger is Driftwood Doug," Roni said. "I think."

"What makes you think that?" Brian asked.

They were walking along Mississippi Avenue toward downtown. The tails of Roni's trenchcoat slapped against her calves in the brisk September breeze. She liked the flapping sound, and wearing the trenchcoat made her feel mysterious and purposeful, like an investigative reporter. Or a spy. And it looked cool.

Brian, on the other hand, was wearing corduroy pants, a

Spider-Man sweatshirt, and a puffy red down vest with feathers leaking from the seams.

Oh well, Roni thought, at least no one will think he's my boyfriend.

She said, "Douglas Unger used to own Bloodwater House, and then he went bankrupt, his wife hanged herself, and he lost the house. I think that was him and his wife in that picture we saw on the boat. And of course Douglas Unger's name is Douglas. As in Doug. As in—"

"—as in Driftwood Doug." Brian finished her thought.

"Exactly!"

"I still don't see how that makes him a kidnapper."

"It makes him a *suspect*."

"But we don't know for sure that was Driftwood Doug in the photo. Also, Alicia was seen getting into an SUV. Driftwood Doug drives a canoe. And let's not forget about Maurice. He drives an SUV, and he was mad because Alicia broke up with him, and he left school early that day."

"We definitely have to talk to Maurice again. But I still think Douglas Unger is our prime suspect."

"My mom seems to think Alicia's real dad is the prime suspect. They'll find him in a day or two, and we'll have wasted our time chasing some bearded boat bum."

Roni stopped walking and turned on Brian. "If you don't want to do this, fine."

"Do *what*?" Brian said. "I don't even know where we're *going*."

"We're going to the hospital." Roni turned her back on him and started walking again.

"Why?" Brian called after her.

"Because, Stink Bomb, it's the scene of the crime."

26

scene of the crime

The trouble with girl reporters, Brian decided, was that they were pushy, irrational, aggressive, dangerous, impulsive, and moody. And that was just for starters. He watched Roni walking away.

This is completely stupid, he thought. He didn't even *know* Alicia Camden. Besides, his mother and the entire Bloodwater police force—not to mention the Goodhue County Sheriff's Department and the highway patrol—were working on Alicia's disappearance twenty-four hours a day.

On the other hand, he thought as he watched Roni's figure grow smaller, yesterday had been one of the most exciting days he'd had since the time his dad had tried to freshen up some stale potato chips in the microwave and the whole thing had gone up in flames and burned half the kitchen down.

Brian frowned. Maybe that wasn't the best example. But he'd learned something about the flammability of potato chips that day. And his mom had gotten a nice new kitchen out of it.

Roni disappeared around the corner of the furniture store on Third Street.

What the heck, Brian thought as he broke into a run. What else was he going to do for the rest of the day?

"Here's the concept," Roni said. "People are creatures of habit. They tend to do the same things at the same time every day. See those two guys in hard hats smoking cigarettes? I bet they stand out there and smoke every day at this time. Probably their lunch hour."

Brian got it right away. "So the people here today at one o'clock might be the same people who were here yesterday at one o'clock. Which was when Alicia got snatched."

"Bravo, Watson."

"Wait a sec. How come I'm Watson?"

"Because I just named you."

"Okay, but I'm not calling you Sherlock." He thought for a second. "Maybe Shirley. Shirley Holmes." He started laughing. He couldn't help it. Sometimes his own jokes just struck him as hilarious, the stupider the better.

Roni didn't even crack a smile. "Very good, Watson."

Brian pulled himself together. At least "Watson" was better than "Stink Bomb." He looked at his watch. One o'clock on the nose.

"Do we question them together, or split up?" he asked.

"Why don't you talk to that nurse sitting on the bench reading a book. I'll deal with the hard hat guys."

"What about the kid in the wheelchair?"

Roni took a look at the boy strapped into the motorized wheelchair parked under the emergency room canopy. "He looks sort of out of it," she said. "I doubt we'll get anything out of him." She started across the parking area toward the two construction workers. Brian shrugged and went to talk to the nurse.

"Excuse me?" he said.

The nurse looked up from her book with a questioning smile. Brian opened his mouth to say more, but nothing came out. This happened to him sometimes with strangers, especially pretty female strangers.

"Are you all right?" asked the nurse.

Brian nodded.

"Are you lost?"

"No! I just wanted to, um, interrogate you." That didn't sound right. "I mean, I wanted to ask you some questions."

The nurse was somehow frowning and smiling and looking beautiful all at the same time.

"About what?" she asked, setting her book on the bench.

"Did you see that girl get abducted yesterday?"

"Who are you?" asked the nurse.

"Brian Bain. I'm . . ." What would Roni say? "I'm interviewing witnesses for an important newspaper article."

"You're a reporter?"

"Not exactly. I'm just sort of helping out a friend." Brian looked across the parking area toward Roni.

"I see," said the nurse, following his glance. "Is that your girlfriend?"

"No!" Brian said. He could feel his face getting hot. "I mean, she's a girl, and she's my friend, but she's not my girlfriend."

"I see." The nurse was grinning.

Brian, desperate to end the conversation, backed away saying, "Okay then, never mind . . ."

"I did see her get into that car," said the nurse.

Brian stopped. "You did? I heard it was an SUV."

"It was one of those jeepy-looking things," said the nurse. "Like a big station wagon."

"That sounds like it could be an SUV."

"I don't know much about cars."

"Did you see the driver?"

"Just the man's arm resting on the window. It was quite hairy. But that's about all I remember. I don't even know what color the car was. SUV, I mean. I mean, I know it wasn't some odd color like pink or purple or chartreuse, because I would have noticed that. It happened very fast. The girl was waiting over there by the curb, the car pulled up, and she got in. I thought nothing of it at the time. Does that help?"

"I think so," said Brian. "Thanks."

"Any time." The nurse picked up her book and continued to read.

"It was one of those Ford Explorers," said the construction worker with the mustache.

"You're either blind or crazy," said the younger, red-headed worker. "It was a GMC Yukon. Either that or a Chevy Tahoe, they look pretty much the same." He pointed his cigarette at Roni. "Don't listen to Brad. He don't know crap."

"Did either of you see the man who was driving?" Roni asked.

Brad said, "I know it was a Ford Explorer on account of my brother drives one just like it."

The redhead dropped his cigarette butt and ground it out with the heel of his steel-toed boot. "You are so full of it, Brad, I don't know how I stand it."

"You can't stand it, you oughta quit bugging me."

"Like I got a choice."

"So neither of you saw the driver?" Roni asked.

Brad said, "No. I saw a green Ford Explorer, and that was it, no matter what this lunkhead tells you."

"It was a white Chevy, you moron. Or a GMC. That's what I told the cops."

The two men glared at each other.

Roni backed away.

Brian was much more comfortable approaching the kid in the wheelchair than he had been talking to the nurse. But he feared Roni was right about this kid. He looked pretty out of it. His head hung off to the side and his eyes were unfocused. One thin hand rested on a small joystick, the other quivered and jerked in midair. He was wearing a Minnesota Twins baseball cap.

Brian said, "Hey."

The kid's head bobbed on his thin neck, then turned toward Brian. His eyes rolled in his head, then seemed to catch on Brian's face.

"Annyong haseyo," the kid said in a creaky voice.

At first Brian thought the kid was talking gibberish. Then he reconfigured the voice and recognized the words from last summer's language camp. A little embarrassed, he had to confess, "Sorry, I don't really speak Korean."

27

chess

Different people see things differently, Roni reminded herself as she left the two hard hats shouting at each other. But this was ridiculous. You would think they could at least agree on the color of the vehicle. She looked around for other potential witnesses and spotted Brian talking to the kid in the wheelchair. Might as well check in with him, she thought.

Brian saw her coming and pointed her out to the wheelchair kid.

"That's my friend Roni, the reporter."

"Pleased to meet you," said the kid in a slow, wavering voice. Roni had to concentrate to make out what he was saying. "My name is Chess."

"As in Chester," Brian explained. "But he plays chess, too."

"Hi, Chess," said Roni. She was surprised the kid could talk.

"I like your coat," said Chess.

"Thanks!" Roni performed a little spin. "Got it at the Goodwill."

"Chess was here yesterday," said Brian.

"I have cerebral palsy," Chess said, head bobbing, left hand hovering and quivering. "Don't worry, it's not contagious."

"He saw the whole thing," Brian said.

"I've been here every day for the past two weeks. My therapy is from eleven to twelve-thirty, so I wait here for my ride."

"You saw Alicia get into the SUV?"

Chess nodded. Or at least she thought it was a nod.

"What kind was it?"

"It was a Jeep Cherokee."

"Oh." Roni frowned. Great. Now she had *three* witnesses, and every one of them saw something completely different.

"It was dark green," said Chess.

At least two of them agreed on the color. Roni said, "I heard it was a Ford Explorer." See how sure this kid was about what he saw.

"There was a green Ford Explorer here, too. And a Chevy Tahoe. But the girl got into the Jeep."

Roni's jaw dropped. "Are you sure?"

"Just because I'm weird looking doesn't mean I can't tell a Jeep from an Explorer."

"Did you see the driver?"

"No."

"Tell her what you told me," said Brian.

Chess looked at Brian and a smile lit up his face. "You mean about the police?"

"Yeah."

"They didn't even bother to talk to me," Chess said.

"Really?"

"Nobody talks to the lump in a wheelchair. Except you guys."

Roni felt herself blush. If it hadn't been for Brian, she might have ignored the kid, too. "Well . . . thanks. This is really good information."

"Any time," said Chess.

They were walking away when Chess called after them. "Hey!"

Roni and Brian stopped and looked back.

Chess said, "Don't you want the license number?"

"Where are you going?" Brian asked.

"Where do you think? We have to report this," Roni said, speeding up. They were walking into the wind. The tails of Roni's trenchcoat flew straight out behind her, flapping in Brian's face.

"I thought you wanted us to be the ones to find her," he said.

"The cops know how to look up license numbers," she said. "They'll find out right away who grabbed Alicia."

"What if we could find her ourselves?"

"How?" She stopped and put her hands on her hips in a stance she must have learned from her mom. "There must be dozens of green Jeeps in Bloodwater."

"But only one with the license number BFLYGUY."

"You know whose Jeep it was?"

"It belongs to Mr. Nestor."

"Who is Mr. Nestor?"

"Mr. Nestor," Brian explained, "is the Butterfly Guy."

28

carnivorous butterflies

Mr. Nestor was a tall, bony man with hairy arms, a bulging forehead, and even bulgier eyes. He answered his door with the perplexed look that most people save for working advanced algebra problems.

"Hi, Mr. Nestor," said Brian. "It's me."

Mr. Nestor stood in the doorway and stared down at the two of them. Brian always had to reintroduce himself. Mr. Nestor knew everything there was to know about insects, but human beings all looked the same to him.

"Who is me?" he asked.

"Brian Bain."

Mr. Nestor fluttered his hands together as if they were wings. "Oh, yes. Oh, my. I remember you. It was swallowtails, wasn't it? Your project?" Brian had met Mr. Nestor for the first time when he had done a seventh-grade science project on swallowtail butterflies.

"That's right. This is my friend Roni," Brian said. "Mind if we come in?"

Mr. Nestor backed into his living room as if they were holding him at gunpoint. "Yes, yes of course."

Brian looked at Roni as they stepped inside. He wanted to see what her face looked like when she saw Mr. Nestor's house. Books were stacked from floor to ceiling. And where there were no books, there were display cases full of dead butterflies. It was a library and a bug museum all squashed into one room.

Roni didn't blink at Mr. Nestor's strange nest. She looked around with open curiosity. "Did you catch all these butterflies?" she asked.

"I've collected from all over the world," said Mr. Nestor. "I captured this particular specimen in Tanzania back in 1994. . . ."

Once Mr. Nestor started talking about his butterflies he could go on for hours, so Brian interrupted him. "Were you at the hospital yesterday?"

"At the hospital?" Mr. Nestor blinked and flapped his hands. "No, I don't believe so. I've been feeling fine."

"Were you anywhere *near* the hospital?" Brian asked.

Mr. Nestor's head swiveled from Roni to Brian. "Let's see. I did drive by the hospital. Yes, indeed. I thought I had seen a Painted American Lady, but it turned out to be a Red Admiral."

Roni gave Brian a puzzled look.

"Those are kinds of butterflies," Brian explained.

Roni said, "Did you pick up a passenger?"

"I believe I did. There was a young lady standing there waiting. She was wearing a scarf that reminded me of a certain Brazilian specimen I once studied, so I asked her if she wanted a lift."

"Where did you take her?"

Mr. Nestor looked blank. He rolled his eyes around in his

head and muttered names of butterflies as if he were chanting.

Finally he said, "I lost her."

"How could you lose a girl?" Brian asked.

"We were driving along when I noticed a Great Spangled Fritillary by the roadside, so I pulled over. Would you like to see it? Very unusual specimen. This has been a good year."

Mr. Nestor would not tell them any more until he showed them his latest butterfly, so they followed him to his specimen room. The Great Spangled Fritillary was an orange and black butterfly about three inches across.

"Isn't it beautiful?" said Mr. Nestor. "Look at how much black is in the wings of this particular specimen. Highly unusual. Remarkable, actually."

"How do you kill them?" Brian asked.

"Formaldehyde. They don't feel a thing. In my hands they achieve immortality. Their beauty will be preserved forever."

"What does this Great Spaniel Literary have to do with Alicia?" Roni asked.

"Who's Alicia?" Mr. Nestor asked.

"The girl you picked up at the hospital!"

"Oh, yes. It took me several minutes to capture this specimen, and when I returned to my vehicle, she was gone."

"Gone?"

"Yes, as if she'd sprouted wings and flown off."

"Where was this?"

"Let's see . . . I'm so bad at directions . . . would you like me to show you?"

"He gives me the creeps," Roni whispered. Mr. Nestor had gone upstairs to search for his car keys.

"He's totally harmless. I think."

"Totally weird, you mean. Maybe he killed Alicia and fed her to a pack of carnivorous butterflies."

Brian laughed. "There are no carnivorous butterflies."

"Maybe he stuck a pin in her and put her in a glass case. Have you ever noticed how many incredibly weird people live in Bloodwater?"

Brian looked pointedly at Roni's green trenchcoat. He looked at the ring in her right nostril.

"I've noticed—" he said, "speaking of weird—that your nose ring used to be in your other nostril."

"It migrated," Roni said.

"I didn't know nose rings could do that."

Roni pulled the fake nose ring from her nostril and put it in her pocket. "There. Is that better?"

Brian cocked his head. "I don't know. I kind of liked it."

Mr. Nestor came clomping down the stairs carrying his car keys in one hand and a butterfly net in the other.

"Are you ready?" he asked.

29

back again

"Look! A Spicebush Swallowtail!" The Jeep swerved over the centerline as Mr. Nestor pointed out the window.

Roni, sitting in the backseat, checked her seat belt.

"Better keep your eye on the road," Brian said.

"Sorry! Sorry!" said Mr. Nestor, bringing the Jeep back under control. They were on the highway just south of Bloodwater. Mr. Nestor kept speeding up and slowing down, his head swiveling back and forth. More than one car had passed them, the drivers leaning angrily on their horns.

"How far is this place?" Roni asked.

"Not far! Not far!"

"I thought you were just giving Alicia a ride home."

"Yes, well, um . . . I don't actually remember where we were going. I only know where we ended up!"

Roni had images of this crazed butterfly hunter driving them to some desolate laboratory and gassing them with formaldehyde. The only thing that kept her from jumping out of the car was the fact that Brian didn't seem to be worried. And the fact that they were going sixty miles per hour. She was thinking about opening the door and bailing out anyway when Mr. Nestor brought the Jeep to an abrupt halt right in the middle of the highway.

"This is the place," he announced.

"This is where you dropped Alicia off?" Roni asked.

"Precisely."

"Why here?"

"This was where I spotted the Great Spangled Fritillary."

"So you just left her here in the middle of nowhere? What did she do?"

"I don't know. I was in pursuit of the Great Spangled! When I returned, the girl was gone."

A semi roared by, horn blaring.

"Maybe you should pull off to the side of the road," Brian suggested.

Mr. Nestor pulled over onto the shoulder and Roni and Brian hopped out. Mr. Nestor grabbed his butterfly net.

"A Hackberry Emperor!" He took off running, swinging his net wildly at a grayish butterfly.

"Look where we are," Brian said. To their left, a grassy field sloped down toward the woods at the edge of the river. He pointed at a narrow dirt track leading across the field. "That's the road to Wolf Spider Island."

"I don't like this," Brian said. "What makes you think she went to the island?"

"She might have gone looking for a phone," Roni said over her shoulder. They were back on the island, following the path that led to Driftwood Doug's houseboat. "Or maybe she just wanted to get away from Mr. Spooky Butterfly Killer back there. And maybe she ran into Driftwood Doug."

"That's a lot of maybes. Maybe she caught a ride back into town."

"Then why is she still missing? It won't hurt to take another look, as long as we're here," Roni said. "Besides, last time we got interrupted."

"Yeah, by a giant hairless troll who wanted to toss me in the river."

"Hoot wouldn't really have dropped you."

"Another maybe."

"Look, we don't know that Driftwood Doug had anything to do with Alicia disappearing, but there has to be some connection. Too many coincidences. Now shut up for a while. We're getting close."

Driftwood Doug's boat came into view a minute later. It looked exactly as they had left it, except that the river had risen a few inches since the storm, and the houseboat now floated level and free. A small fire was burning in the fire pit on shore. Roni walked up to the fire pit and looked into it.

"What are you looking for?" Brian whispered as he walked up next to her and stared into what appeared to be a normal campfire.

"Evidence. He might be burning Alicia's clothes."

Brian shuddered. Sometimes Roni completely creeped him out.

"Don't worry, it's just wood," Roni said. She started toward the boat.

Brian said, "I got a bad feeling about this."

Ignoring him, Roni hopped onto the deck and peered through one of the portholes.

"See anything?" Brian asked.

Roni shook her head and rapped on the glass. "Anybody home?" she called out.

No answer.

"Come on," Brian said. "Let's get out of here."

"Just a minute," Roni said.

"What if Hoot shows up again?" Brian did not like this situation at all. He looked down at the fire. Why would Driftwood Doug leave a fire burning unattended?

"There's nobody in here," Roni said. She sounded disappointed. Brian was relieved.

"Then let's *go*!" he said. Just then he heard a twig snap. For a second he froze. Then he turned around slowly and looked up.

Brian's first impression was that an enormous bundle of sticks was walking toward him. Just as he realized that he was looking at a man carrying a load of firewood, the man dropped his load of branches and twigs with a crash, and Brian got his first close-up look at Driftwood Doug.

driftwood doug

Driftwood Doug up close looked a lot like Driftwood Doug from far away, only hairier. His reddish-brown beard covered about two-thirds of his face and hung down over his throat. Dark brown hair exploded from his skull in a riot of coils and spikes. His blue eyes stood out like radioactive sapphires.

"Well, well," said Driftwood Doug, crossing his arms. "Are you the burglars Hoot told me about?" He was wearing his usual denim bib overalls over a red-checked flannel shirt.

"No," said Brian.

"Yes," said Roni.

Driftwood Doug looked from Brian to Roni, and back again. "Well? Are you or aren't you?"

"We're not burglars," Brian said quickly.

"It was a misunderstanding," Roni added. "We just wanted to talk to you."

"Is that so," said Driftwood Doug. He bent over and threw a few pieces of wood into the fire, sending a spray of sparks into the air. "Why would you want to talk to me?"

"We're investigating the disappearance of Alicia Camden," Roni said. "She was last seen in this area."

Brian was impressed. He knew Roni must be as scared as

he was, but she sounded fearless. He watched Driftwood Doug carefully, but the man didn't seem surprised by Roni's question.

"Alicia Camden?" He picked up a limb the size of a baseball bat and used it to stir the fire. "The girl who lives at Bloodwater House?"

"Yes," Roni said, hopping down from the pontoon. "Have you seen her?"

"Do you mean here? On the island?"

Roni nodded.

Driftwood Doug's sapphire eyes glittered. His shoulders tensed and his hand tightened around the limb. Brian thought, Uh-oh, he's deciding how he's going to kill us and where he's going to hide our bodies. He braced himself to take off running.

Driftwood Doug threw the stick into the fire.

"That poor girl," he said, shaking his head sorrowfully. His shoulders dropped a few inches and his body sagged. In a single instant he went from being a fearsome, hairy, club-wielding giant to a normal, worried man. "If not for me, this would never have happened. That poor, poor girl!"

Brian and Roni gaped at him. Was this a confession? Was Driftwood Doug *confessing* to them?

"Where is she?" Roni asked. "Where did you put her?"

"Put her? I didn't put her anywhere. I haven't seen her since last Friday."

"But . . . you kidnapped her, right?" Roni reminded him.

"Kidnapped? Don't be ridiculous!"

"Then what happened to her?" Brian asked.

"The same thing that happened to me," said Driftwood Doug. "I once owned Bloodwater House, you know."

"So you *are* Douglas Unger?"

"I *was* Douglas Unger. Until that house destroyed me. It was the Bloodwater Curse."

"The *what*?" said Roni and Brian together.

Driftwood Doug looked from one to the other, then said, "Would you care for a cup of tea?"

tea for three

"Sugar?" Driftwood Doug asked as he poured the hot tea. They were sitting around the fire, which Doug had used to heat water for the tea.

Roni said, "Yes, please." She let the earthy aroma of the tea drift toward her while stirring in her sugar.

Brian sniffed his tea as if it were a science experiment. "You aren't trying to poison us, are you?"

Driftwood Doug grinned. The smile changed his whole look. Suddenly a set of perfect white teeth showed through his beard, and his skin crinkled around his eyes.

"I'm fresh out of poison today," he said.

"What is this?" Brian asked.

"Elixir of the gods," said Driftwood Doug.

"I don't think I've ever had elixir of the gods before," said Brian.

"What is it really?" Roni asked.

Driftwood Doug took a big healthy gulp of the tea. "Have you ever heard of ginseng?"

Roni had heard of it. "You mean that stuff that gives you extra energy?"

"I know, I know." Brian was waving his hand as if they were in school. "It's a root, right?"

Roni remembered seeing the pile of dried roots on the

table inside the houseboat. Those must have been ginseng roots.

Driftwood Doug nodded. "You are both right. Ginseng root is said to give one extra strength and vitality. It grows wild in the woods around here. I earn money in the fall by collecting and selling ginseng roots."

Brian took a big swallow of his tea. He made a face, then took another sip.

Roni said, "Are you going to tell us about Alicia?" She tasted her tea. Not bad.

"The girl, yes," said Driftwood Doug. "I saw her last Friday when I was hunting for chanterelles."

"What are those?" Brian asked.

Roni had to teach him to not lead a suspect off the track when she started a line of questioning.

"Cantharellus cibarius," said Driftwood Doug, as if that explained something. "The most delectable of the wild mushrooms."

Roni said, "Okay, you were looking for these cantrels—"

"Chanterelles," he corrected her.

"These mushrooms, and then?"

Driftwood Doug was not to be hurried. "I'd had some luck finding chanterelles in the woods near Bloodwater House. I picked nearly five pounds there last August. Not to mention a nice patch of *Boletus edulis* . . ."

This guy is as bad as Mr. Nestor, Roni thought.

" . . . and of course I'm always keeping an eye out for ginseng. That night the sun had set and I was cutting through the woods in the dark, heading back to where I'd stashed my canoe, when I heard shouting coming from the direction of the house. I stopped and listened, but I couldn't make anything out. Then I heard a screech."

"A screech?" Roni said.

"Like a shout of pain. Or maybe anger. I don't know. I thought maybe someone had been hurt, so I started for the house. It's the Curse, you know. Terrible things happen to people who live there. Anyway, I was almost to the fence when someone came running from the direction of the house and jumped the fence and took off through the woods. He ran past me, not twenty feet away."

"Did you see who it was?"

"Like I said, it was getting dark and I couldn't see much. It was a young man, I believe. Quite tall."

Brian looked at Roni and silently moved his mouth. Roni could read his lips: *Maurice.* She nodded.

"He ran toward the river," said Driftwood Doug. "So I crept up to the back fence. That was when I saw the girl. On her hands and knees on the patio near the pool. A man was standing over her."

"Could you see who it was?" Roni asked.

"I believe it was Arnold Thorn."

"Did he hit her?"

"When I saw him he was just standing there talking to her. Then he tried to grab her, like he wanted to help her stand up, but she knocked his hand aside and crawled away. The man followed her and tried to help her up again, but she wouldn't let him. He just stood there looking at her for a while, then a woman's voice called from the house and he ran back inside. As soon as he was gone, the girl got up. Her face was all bloody. She ran around the side of the house and that was the last I saw her. A few seconds later Arnold Thorn came back outside and started looking for her and calling her name."

"Then what?"

"Then nothing. I left."

"You didn't do anything?" Brian asked.

"What should I have done?"

"Called the police."

"I was trespassing. I didn't want to get in trouble." He stared into his tea. "I tried to warn him, you know. When Arnold Thorn first bought that house I tried to warn him of the Curse. He wouldn't listen. He told me to get off his property. He called the police. I should have burned that house down after Ceci died. I should have burned it to the ground." He stared off into the distance. "Before we bought that place, we were happy. A few months later all my investments went bad, Ceci died, and I gave it all up. I became Driftwood Doug."

He looked up and suddenly his expression changed. Roni turned and saw two uniformed policemen coming quickly up the path.

32

firth and spall

Brian saw the police at the same time Roni did. He recognized both of them—George Firth, a potbellied old-timer with the Bloodwater police, and Garth Spall, a brash young cop whom Brian had once overheard his mother describe as "Barney Fife in Arnold Schwarzenegger's body."

This is perfect timing, Brian thought. Now Doug can tell the police what he saw. But when Brian turned back to the fire, Driftwood Doug was gone. Brian jumped up and looked around and saw Doug down at the shore pushing his canoe out onto the river.

The younger cop, Garth Spall, saw him, too. He grabbed Firth's arm and pointed, then went crashing through the brush toward the canoe, holding his flopping gunbelt and shouting, "Stop! Stop! Police!"

Doug hopped into his canoe and began to paddle.

Spall reached the water's edge and threw himself headlong at the canoe. He landed with a tremendous splash about five feet short of the canoe. Driftwood Doug pulled away, paddling furiously. Spall came up sputtering in the knee-deep water, fumbling with his sodden holster. "Stop or I'll shoot!" He got his gun out just as Firth caught up with him and grabbed his arm.

"You can't *shoot* him, Garth."

"I was just going to throw a scare into him," Spall said, lowering his gun. Driftwood Doug disappeared from sight along the shore.

"Well, you sure threw a scare into me!" said Firth. "We didn't come here to *shoot* the man, Garth! Just ask him a few questions."

"He ran. He must be guilty," Garth said stubbornly.

"That doesn't mean you're supposed to *shoot* him!"

Garth Spall reholstered his gun and pushed out his lower lip like a little kid. "You don't always have to tell me what to do."

"Oh for . . . look, why don't you head back to the bridge and see if you can catch sight of where he's headed. He has to put into shore someplace. Meanwhile, I'll talk to his accomplices here. And no shooting!"

The two cops waded back to shore. Garth shook himself like a dog, sending water droplets in every direction, then pounded off down the narrow path, his broad, wet shoulders parting the brush as he passed. Firth looked back at Brian and Roni, who were still standing next to the campfire holding their teacups.

"We aren't accomplices," Brian said.

"Is that a fact?" said Firth. He waddled up and took a closer look at Brian. "Aren't you Annie Bain's boy?"

Brian nodded.

The cop shook his head. "Well, I'm sure she'll be happy to

113

know we found you here on Wolf Spider Island keeping company with Mr. Douglas Unger." He turned his attention to Roni. "And who might you be, young lady?"

Roni did not like being young-ladied. She pulled out her notebook and clicked her pen. "I'm P. Q. Delicata, reporter for the *Bloodwater Pump*." She looked at the cop's name badge. "What is your interest in Douglas Unger, Officer Firth? And why did your partner try to shoot him?"

"Whoa!" said Firth, holding up his palms. "Now just hold your horses, Miss P. Q. Delicata. Nobody shot at nobody. We came here to ask Mr. Unger some questions is all."

"In connection with the Alicia Camden kidnapping?" Roni asked.

Firth narrowed his eyes. "I know you—you're the girl trying to get into Bloodwater House yesterday!"

Just then, Firth's belt radio erupted.

"I see him! I see him! Heading south on river! Am in pursuit!"

Firth grabbed his radio and shouted into it. "Garth, you moron, do not—I repeat—do NOT unholster your weapon!" He gave Roni and Brian an exasperated look. "I'll deal with you two later." He returned his radio to his belt clip and ran off down the path, his abdomen jiggling like a sack of Jell-O.

donuts and coffee

"I wonder if they'll catch him," Roni said as they trudged into Bloodwater.

"I doubt it," said Brian. "I bet Doug knows every little backwater and inlet from here to Alma."

"Good point. But I wonder why he ran. He sure didn't sound like a kidnapper when we were talking to him."

"Yeah, he made it sound more like it was either Maurice or Mr. Thorn that beat up Alicia."

"But then why did he run?" Roni asked.

"Good question. Any ideas?"

"Yes. Let's eat," Roni said.

Brian stared at her. He never knew what she was going to say next.

"I think better if I have a little sustenance," she explained.

"I thought you were on a diet."

"Which I will temporarily abandon for the sake of this investigation."

"Fine by me." They were walking side by side, kicking stones at the edge of the road. "Do you have any money?"

"I have five bucks. How about you?"

"I have a couple of dollars. What do you want to eat?"

Roni's eyes lit up. "Let's go to Bratten's. Today is French donut day—my favorite."

"That doesn't sound like lunch."

"It's the new all-carbohydrate-and-fat diet," Roni said.

At Bratten's Café and Bakery, Roni ordered three French donuts and a cup of coffee. Brian ordered one French donut and one American donut, just in case the French donut was too froufrou for him. He also ordered a cup of coffee.

"You kids grow up too fast," said Mrs. Bratten as she rang up their purchases.

Brian had never ordered a cup of coffee in a restaurant. For that matter, he had never had a cup of coffee at home. The few times he had tasted his dad's coffee he hadn't liked it. Too hot and bitter and sour. But it seemed the thing to do when you were eating donuts out in public while working on a big investigation. Besides, he didn't want Roni to think he was a little kid.

They took their coffee and donuts to one of the small tables by the front window. Roni bit into her first French donut. "Now *this*," she said, munching, "is elixir of the gods."

"Doesn't an elixir have to be a liquid?"

"Shut up and eat," she said.

Brian did, taking a huge bite from his French donut. Roni was right. Elixir of the gods, even if it was a solid. He watched Roni pour cream into her coffee and then add a packet of sugar. It was worth a try. He poured in a slug of cream, which changed the color of his coffee from black to beige, then tore the tops from two packets of sugar and dumped them in. He stirred. He lifted it to his lips and tasted.

Hmm, not bad. Kind of like burnt hot chocolate. He added another dollop of cream and two more sugars. Even better.

Halfway through her second donut, Roni said, "Okay, let's assume that Driftwood Doug abducted Alicia. The question is, *why?*"

"Love, money, or revenge," Brian said.

"He didn't seem like a love, money, or revenge sort of guy."

"I agree. And why would he tell us that story about seeing Alicia with Mr. Thorn?"

"Maybe he was lying about what he saw. Or maybe he kidnapped Alicia to protect *her* from *them.*"

"Now, that's completely crazy," Brian said.

"We already know he's crazy. All that Bloodwater Curse nonsense."

"Maybe it's not nonsense. Just about everybody who ever lived in that house died. And crazy doesn't necessarily mean guilty." Brian took another gulp of coffee. The top of his head was vibrating. He could grow to like the stuff.

"The only thing we know for sure is that Alicia got beat up last Friday," Roni said. "If Doug was telling us the truth, then Alicia got beat up in her own backyard by Mr. Thorn, or by the guy that Driftwood Doug saw running away."

"Who was probably Maurice."

"So if it was Maurice or Mr. Thorn who hit her, she was lying to the police when she told them a stranger had attacked her in the park."

"Which makes no sense at all."

"Sure it does. Alicia might have been covering. I've heard of kids doing that. She didn't want anybody to know that her stepdad was a jerk, or that her boyfriend beat her up. Maybe Little Miss Perfect Tennis Star Alicia wanted everyone to think her life was all peaches and cream."

Brian sat back. "Me-ow," he said, clawing the air like a cat.

"Shut *up*!" Roni scowled. Then she laughed. "Okay, she bugs me a little." Roni took out her notebook. "Let's lay it out. Who are all the possible suspects?"

Brian said, "First, there's Mr. Thorn."

Roni wrote Thorn's name at the top of the page. "But why would he kidnap his own daughter?"

"The Curse drove him insane."

"You mention that curse one more time and you'll drive *me* insane. Seriously, why would Mr. Thorn snatch his own stepdaughter?"

"Maybe she was going to report him for child abuse."

"A possibility. Who else?"

"Maurice. Because he's a jerk and he's in love with her and he couldn't stand it that she broke up with him. An *if-I-can't-have-you-then-nobody-can* thing. He lied about being in class that afternoon, so he must be covering up something."

"Who else have we got?"

"There's Alicia's real father in Mankato. My mom thinks he's the prime suspect. Real dads are always stealing their kids."

Roni wrote that down in her notebook.

"And, of course, Driftwood Doug," Brian said.

Roni added Driftwood Doug and a few more names to her list.

Brian read the three new names she had written: Mr. Nestor, Tyrone Eakin, and Mysterious Stranger.

"Why Tyrone?" he asked.

"Maurice thought Tyrone had a thing for Alicia. That was why he keyed Tyrone's car."

"Oh. And Mysterious Stranger?"

"Just what it says."

"What about your buddy Hoot?"

"Hoot wouldn't kidnap anybody."

"Write him down anyway. How many have we got?"

Roni frowned at the list of names. "Too many," she said.

"Who's your favorite?"

Roni pushed out her lips and stared at the list.

"My personal favorite? Maurice is pretty cute . . ."

Brian had just taken a big gulp of coffee and at the final two words, a laugh exploded from his belly, sending coffee up his throat and out his nose and across the table in a milky spray, which made him start coughing and laugh even harder. Roni wiped off the piece of paper and then she too started laughing. At first it was a small tremor, but then it gathered force and became an all-out guffaw.

They were surprised and a little offended when, a few seconds later, Mrs. Bratten walked up to their table and asked them to leave.

"Come back when you've grown up enough to behave yourselves," she said.

34

money pit

"That was certainly humiliating," Roni said.

"At least she let us keep our donuts."

"Of course she did. We paid for them, didn't we?"

"I guess." Brian reached into the bag for his second donut, a chocolate-frosted, glazed-raised with sprinkles.

They walked for a few minutes without talking. Brian ate his donut slowly, his jaw working in time with his feet. Roni, fists buried in the pockets of her trenchcoat, was lost in thought. But she seemed to know where she was going.

Brian finished his donut, then asked, "You really think Maurice is cute?"

"Of course he is."

"So do you *like* him?"

"Of course not."

"Would you go out with him if he asked you?"

"If I wanted to go out with him *I'd* ask *him*."

"Oh." Brian licked his chocolatey fingers. "Are you gonna?"

Roni stopped abruptly. "Are you stupid, dense, or half-witted?"

"Are those my only choices?"

"Yes." She started walking again, faster this time.

"Where are you taking me this time?" Brian scrambled to keep up.

"To find some answers."

"Where? Are we going to Maurice's house?"

Roni laughed. "Where did you learn to be so irritating?"

"From my mom."

"Figures."

"So where are we going?" Brian asked again, although he thought he knew the answer.

"I'll give you one guess."

A few minutes later they were standing outside the fence surrounding Bloodwater House.

"Did you know that Driftwood Doug's wife hanged herself from this fence?" Roni asked.

"I've read about that," Brian said. "But I didn't know she was Driftwood Doug's wife until today."

"I wouldn't want to be a cop," Roni said. "Way too much yuck potential."

"I think you get used to the spattered blood and guts after a while."

Roni made a face. "No thank you. My mom's meat loaf is as close to blood and guts as I want to get. In fact, I don't even want to get *that* close."

"Are you going to tell me what we're doing here?"

"We're going to interview Ted Thorn. I want to find out if Arnold Thorn is the sort of man who would beat up his own daughter. You press the buzzer on the gate and see if you can get Ted to open up."

"What about you?"

"I'm afraid if Mrs. Thorn sees me she'll pop a gasket. I'll sneak around back and wait by the swimming pool. You and Ted can meet me there."

After Ted Thorn buzzed the gate open, Brian marched straight up to the front door while Roni followed the flagstone path through the side garden that led to the back of the lot. Looking at the carefully trimmed hedges, the weedless pathway, and the precisely ordered rows of rosebushes, Roni wondered how expensive it must be to maintain such perfection. Maybe it was worth it. The roses must be beautiful in season.

She looked up at the house, at the limestone walls, the leaded glass windows, the gables, the slate roof. There was no other house like it in Bloodwater. No other house even half so impressive. How many rooms did it have? At least thirty. Maybe fifty.

But the house itself was far from perfect. The stone walls were cracked and stained. Several of the windows were missing panes, and had been patched with plastic and tape. And the old iron gutters and downspouts had long since rusted through.

Nick had called the place a "money pit," and had suggested that the Thorns were just about broke. Roni wondered why they had spent their time and money on the garden when the house itself needed so much work. Maybe it was all they could afford to do.

Or maybe they were driven mad by the Bloodwater Curse.

If there was such a thing.

Which there wasn't.

Roni came around the back corner of the house onto the patio where only yesterday she had nearly been attacked by Mrs. Thorn. Maybe things would go better today. She walked to the edge of the pool and stared down into the water.

She wondered if Alicia would ever turn up. Every year, teenage girls disappeared, never to be found.

I never got a chance to apologize for beating her up, Roni thought.

"Well, well. Who do we have here?"

Roni whirled and almost fell into the pool.

"Careful now," said Arnold Thorn, reaching out a hand to steady her.

arnold thorn

Roni shook off his hand and backed away.

Mr. Thorn chuckled. "I didn't mean to startle you."

"That's okay."

"You're one of Alicia's friends, I take it?"

"That's right. Have you heard from her?"

"I'm afraid not." Thorn reached into his breast pocket and brought out a flat gold cigarette case. He opened the lid, took out a cigarette, fitted it to his thin lips, and lit it with a matching gold lighter. This was Roni's first good look at Alicia's stepdad. The last time she'd seen him there had been too much going on.

Arnold Thorn should have been a handsome man. His features were regular, his hair was thick and blond, his eyes were blue, and he had a trim physique. He wore a soft gray suit and a pair of gray lizardskin loafers. His problem was that he looked *too* perfect. His smile had an artificial curve, as if it were painted on, and even his flawless skin had the smooth plasticky look of a store mannequin. A scar would have improved his appearance considerably.

Roni could see where Ted Thorn had learned his wrinkle-free ways.

She said, "I hope she turns up soon. Everybody's really worried about her. But I hear the police have a suspect."

"They do?" He glanced around, then fixed her with a hard stare. "The police need to keep us better informed. Who is this suspect?"

Roni couldn't think of a reason not to tell him. "Driftwood Doug," she said.

Thorn looked at her sharply. His eyes were an opaque, impenetrable blue, as if they had been painted on. Like his smile.

"That disgusting derelict? How do you know so much?" he asked, squinting at her through a veil of cigarette smoke. He wasn't smiling anymore.

Roni tried to imagine this elegant mannequin man punching Alicia in the face. She looked at his hands. In his left hand he held his cigarette loosely between his long fingers. His right hand was in his pocket.

Roni took half a step back. She wished Brian and Ted would show up.

"I have friends in the police department," she said.

Mr. Thorn took a step toward her. "And they think this Driftwood fellow had something to do with Alicia's disappearance?"

"Did you know he used to own this place?" Roni said quickly.

"Who?"

"Douglas Unger. Otherwise known as Driftwood Doug."

"He did?"

"Yes. Ten years ago."

Mr. Thorn looked at her for several seconds, then flicked

his cigarette to the patio and ground it out with the tip of a lizardskin loafer.

"You know a great deal for such a little girl," he said.

Roni took another half step back, which put her at the edge of the pool. She could feel her heart beating. If she yelled, would they hear her from inside the house? Where were Brian and Ted? Mr. Thorn loomed over her. If he got any closer she would have to jump in the pool.

Roni whipped out her notebook and clicked her pen and said, "Would you care to comment on the rumor that you like to beat up girls?"

That made him take a step back. *"What?"* His face darkened. "What did you say?"

"I heard you beat up Alicia. Is it true?"

"That is a vicious lie!" he said—but the mannequin mask slipped, and for a moment Roni saw straight through those opaque blue eyes.

She saw that he was afraid.

perfect pitch

Inside Bloodwater House, Brian and Ted encountered some difficulties of their own. Namely, the formidable Mrs. Thorn.

"You—" She directed her laser gaze toward Brian. "You're a friend of that awful fat girl!"

"She's not fat," Brian mumbled, averting his eyes.

"What did you say?"

Brian pretended Mrs. Thorn was a face in a video game. It helped.

"I said she's not really fat. She just likes to wear loose clothes."

"You have a smart mouth on you, young man. Well, you can just take that smart mouth and march it right out of this house this instant!" Boy, was she ever appropriately named. She was one of the prickliest people he'd ever met.

"Mom . . . ," Ted began, but his voice trailed off.

Brian decided that retreat was in order. He backed away, saying, "I'll see you *soon,* Ted. *Soon.*" He headed for the front door, hoping that Ted would get the message and meet him and Roni out back.

Brian walked quickly down the walk to the front gate, which clicked and swung open as he approached it. Mrs. Thorn must be watching from the house, he thought. He turned down Riverview Terrace and walked until he was out of sight behind a lilac hedge. He stopped and waited for a few seconds, then cut through the hedge and followed the iron fence to the back gate. Using his Swiss Army knife, Brian slipped the gate lock and entered the back garden.

There was a moment when Roni thought it had worked. Mr. Thorn was so surprised by her accusation that he took a step back. She clicked her pen and pretended to write something in her notebook.

"What are you writing?" Mr. Thorn said. The slick friendliness in his voice was gone, replaced by something that sounded more like a choking dog.

"I'm working on a story," Roni replied.

"Let me see." Mr. Thorn reached for the notebook.

Roni held the notebook out of his reach, but when she put her foot back to brace herself, there was nothing there. She had forgotten that she was standing at the edge of the pool. She flailed her arms, trying to regain her balance. Mr. Thorn grabbed her by the hand, the one holding the notebook. Instinctively, Roni kicked out. Her boot connected solidly with his shin. He let out a roar and let go, and Roni hit the water, still clutching her notebook. When she surfaced, sputtering and coughing, she saw Mr. Thorn hopping up and down on one leg, holding his shin.

Just then there was a sound, like a hammer hitting a coconut. Mr. Thorn's expression went blank and something struck the patio with a dull clunk. Thorn's mouth fell open and his fists relaxed and a bright splotch of blood appeared on his forehead. He teetered for an endless instant, then toppled.

Brian, standing on the other side of the pool, could not believe what he had done.

When he saw Mr. Thorn throw Roni into the pool, he had gone on automatic and grabbed the nearest thing he could find—an egg-size rock from the garden.

Maybe I'll startle him, he had thought. Give Roni a chance to get away.

He had brought his arm back and thrown the stone as hard as he could, never dreaming that it would actually hit its target. But the rock had sailed straight and true across the pool to hit Mr. Thorn smack on the forehead. The best throw of his life. It had made a sound he would never forget.

And then Roni had screamed.

That was another sound he would never forget.

Roni hadn't known she could scream like that. The sound had poured from her throat like a shriek from a horror movie. They must have heard her half a mile away.

And suddenly Brian was there, helping her out of the pool.

"Are you okay?" Brian asked.

"I'm okay, but somebody shot Mr. Thorn!" Roni cried.

"No, they didn't." Brian bent over Mr. Thorn. "I threw a rock at him."

"You what?"

"I think he's breathing."

"You threw a what?"

"A rock. Listen, we gotta call an ambulance or something."

Suddenly, Roni's mind went from utterly bewildered to crystal clear. She knew what she had to do. She grabbed Brian by the arm.

"You have to get out of here, Brian. Right now!"

"But—"

"Shut up and don't argue. I'll take care of Mr. Thorn. You get out of here. Now!"

Brian wavered, his eyes going back to the man lying senseless on the patio.

"Now!" Roni shouted.

Brian turned and ran out through the back gate and into the woods.

37

fleeing

About one second after Brian disappeared into the woods, Mrs. Thorn came charging out of the house. When she saw Mr. Thorn sprawled on the patio with Roni bending over him, she let out a shriek that made Roni's hair stand on end.

"Get away from him!" Mrs. Thorn shouted, running toward her.

Roni stood up. "He's hurt," she said. "We should call 911."

Mrs. Thorn pushed Roni away and stared down at her unconscious husband.

"You killed him!" she said.

"He's not dead," Roni said. "We should call an ambulance."

Mrs. Thorn seemed not to hear her.

"Mrs. Thorn?" Roni said.

Mrs. Thorn was just standing there like a zombie, not hearing her at all.

Roni ran to the house and let herself in. She ran through the echoey halls from room to room looking for a phone. Nearly all the rooms were empty—not a stick of furniture in them. She finally found a phone in an alcove near the front door, called 911, then ran back to the pool, where she found Mrs. Thorn on her knees holding her husband's bleeding head in her lap.

"I called 911," Roni said. "An ambulance should be here in a few minutes."

Mrs. Thorn looked up at Roni and said, "You're going to jail for this, you horrid, horrid girl."

"I don't think so," Roni said. "I was only defending myself."

"I'll have you put away for the rest of your sorry life!"

"And I'll have *him* arrested for assault," Roni shouted, losing it. "He was the one who beat up Alicia—and he was about to beat me up, too!"

Mrs. Thorn's pink face turned white. She let go of her husband and stood up. Mr. Thorn flopped back down, the back of his head bouncing on the patio.

"You . . . don't . . . know . . . *anything,*" Mrs. Thorn said in a nasty, brittle voice. But Roni could see that she'd hit a nerve.

Just then, Mr. Thorn moaned and his eyes snapped open. He sat up, blood running down his face and onto his perfect suit, blinking and looking back and forth with a bewildered, cross-eyed look. Then his eyes fixed on Roni.

"My goodness," he said. "You're soaking wet!"

Brian didn't know he could run so fast. Branches whipped his face, brambles tore at his skin, and he tripped over logs on the ground, but he kept going. After running for what felt like hours—but he knew in his logical, scientific mind was probably only about five minutes—he ran out of steam.

Gasping for breath, he sank down to the ground beneath a towering cottonwood and tried to figure out where he was. The strip of woodland between Riverview Terrace and the river was only about one square mile in size, but it was easy to get turned around in the maze of coulees and hummocks and moss-covered boulders. He thought he could make out the river through the trees, but the woods were so dense he couldn't be sure.

After catching his breath, he stood up and tried to make a plan. He couldn't go back the way he'd come. He wondered how Roni was making out with the Thorns. He hoped Mr. Thorn was okay. Could a little rock like that kill a man? Brian felt sick thinking about it. He hadn't meant to hurt anybody.

He decided to head straight for the river. There was a path leading along the shore that ran all the way from Riverfront Park to Barn Bluff. He could follow the path to Barn Bluff, which was only a few blocks from his home.

He hoped there wouldn't be a squad of police—led by his mother—waiting there to arrest him.

Brian made his way toward the river, carefully descending a steep, narrow gully that widened into a coulee. Had he actually been running through these woods? He was lucky he hadn't killed himself.

This was all Roni's fault. Once again, he was in trouble, worse trouble than he had ever been in before in his life, and it was because of Roni. She was the one who had wanted to go back to Bloodwater House. Brian was starting to think the Bloodwater Curse didn't just apply to the owners, but to anyone who came in contact with the place.

A few minutes later the coulee widened. Brian found

himself on a narrow path just a few yards from the edge of the river. He turned right. Barn Bluff couldn't be more than a ten-minute walk—if this was the right path.

Brian had gone only a few yards when he heard a strange sound.

He froze. It sounded like an animal. Maybe an owl. Or a sick bobcat.

Or somebody crying.

Slowly, he moved along the path, placing each foot down gently so he didn't make any noise. The path made a sharp turn around a boulder the size of minivan. He peeked around it and gulped. Sitting on a fallen log was a girl with long dirty hair, mud-smeared cheeks, black circles around her eyes, and clothing that looked like it had been dragged behind a plow. She turned her huge eyes toward him, opened her mouth, jumped to her feet, and shrieked.

Brian heard a yelp come out of his own mouth at the same time. They both backed away from each other, then stopped.

"Who are you?" the girl asked.

"Brian Bain." She had asked him a question that he knew the answer to. Not that the answer would mean anything to her. "Are you hurt?"

The girl shook her head as if his question was impossibly complex.

"Do you know where we are?" she asked.

"Sort of," said Brian. "Barn Bluff is up that way, I think. Where are you trying to get to?"

"Do you know how to get to Bloodwater House?"

"Sure! You just . . ." Brian's eyes went wide. "Why do you want to go there?" Even as the question came out of his mouth, Brian realized who he was talking to, and he knew what her answer would be.

"Because I live there," said Alicia.

lost and found

"Everybody's been looking for you," the kid said. "Did someone kidnap you?"

With each step Alicia thought her legs were about to crumble. She had never been so tired in her entire life. All she could think about was how good it would feel to sink into her own soft, dry mattress.

"So what happened to you, anyway?" The kid just wouldn't shut up. What was his name? He had told her, but she couldn't remember. Bruce? Brent? Bryce?

"I don't want to talk about it," she mumbled, forcing her feet to keep moving, one step after another. How many hours had it been since she had awakened on the riverbank, soaking wet, bruised, and covered with insect bites? How many miles had she walked?

"The police are still looking for you. You and Driftwood Doug."

Alicia stopped walking. "Driftwood Doug?" She imagined his dark, hairy face and shuddered.

"Yeah. They figured he abducted you because he'd been hanging around your house. But when the police tried to question him he took off in his canoe."

Alicia started walking again. "How much farther?" she

asked. She imagined Driftwood Doug hiding behind every tree and bush.

"Not far."

"I suppose everybody is worried."

"I'd say so. The police, your parents, everybody. What happened to you, anyway?"

Alicia stopped and closed her eyes. "I was on a boat. Locked in the cabin. I couldn't leave."

"Wow," the kid said. "How'd you get away?"

Alicia heard the words come tumbling out of her mouth. "This storm came up. It was awful. The boat was tied up on Wolf Spider Island, but the wind tore it loose. I kicked the cabin door open. Then the boat hit a tree and I got thrown off and I swam to shore. I guess I must have passed out or something, because when I woke up I was lying in the mud getting bit by flies, and it wasn't night anymore, it was the middle of the day. I started walking. I got to the road and hiked back toward town. But I didn't want anybody to see me like this so I decided to cut through the woods and—" She opened her eyes. "I got lost."

"Who locked you on the boat? Was it Driftwood Doug?"

Alicia looked around, imagining faces in the trees, like the devil face carved in the tree on Wolf Spider Island, and suddenly she felt afraid—even more afraid than she had been on the boat in the storm. She squeezed her eyes shut again and tried to imagine herself back in Mankato, back in their little house with her real dad. Back before her mom had met Arnold Thorn. But no matter how hard she tried to magic herself back to Mankato, she knew when she opened her eyes she would still be standing in the woods with this weird little kid Byron, or Bruno, or whatever his name was.

"Alicia?"

Alicia lifted her eyelids. The kid was staring right into her face.

"Come on," he said. "Let's get you home."

Roni had just about gotten everything taken care of with the Thorns by the time they heard the howl of the ambulance in the distance. Mr. Thorn, who remembered nothing, believed Roni's story that he had fallen and hit his head. Mrs. Thorn had calmed down enough to go along with the story as well. She seemed to understand that if she accused Roni of attacking her husband, Roni might accuse Mr. Thorn of attacking her, and things might get very ugly.

Roni was sure that the Thorns were covering up something, and she was pretty sure she knew what it was—Mr. Thorn was the one who had beaten Alicia. Maybe he had even kidnapped his own stepdaughter and stashed her someplace to keep her from talking.

But at the moment, Arnold Thorn did not look much like a dangerous kidnapper. He was holding a wet towel to his head while Mrs. Thorn tried to get him to drink some water. They both seemed to have forgotten about Roni. Maybe she should sneak inside the house and do a search right now, while the Thorns were distracted. She started toward the back door and was almost inside when she heard Mrs. Thorn emit another screech.

Roni turned and saw the Thorns staring across the pool at two figures coming in through the back gate. One of them was Brian Bain. The other one was a dirty, bedraggled, tired-looking girl. Roni thought she recognized the girl, but she couldn't quite believe it.

Arnold Thorn climbed unsteadily to his feet. He held out his arms, one hand still holding the bloody towel, and started toward the girl. "Alicia?"

Alicia stepped to the side, avoiding his embrace. Mr. Thorn dropped his arms. Alicia walked around him.

Mrs. Thorn ran up to Alicia and stared at her. "Oh my God! What's happened to you?"

Alicia looked back at her mother, her eyes hard, her lips squeezed into a short, tight line.

"Alicia?" Mrs. Thorn took her daughter's shoulders in her hands. "Are you okay?"

Alicia shook her head. Her mouth quivered and loosened, and her eyes filled up, and she leaned into her mother's shoulder and began to cry.

"Who did this to you?" Mrs. Thorn asked.

"It was awful," Alicia sobbed.

"Who, baby? Who?"

"It was that man, that hairy man that spies on us from the woods. Driftwood Doug! He locked me on the boat and he wouldn't let me out!" Alicia's voice rose to a hysterical wail. Sobbing and pounding on her mother's shoulders with her fists, she cried, "I couldn't get out!"

three pounds

MISSING STUDENT FOUND

Alicia Camden made it back home Tuesday afternoon. She was discovered in the woods near her home by a fellow student.

"She was only a few hundred yards from her home," said Bloodwater High student Brian Bain.

The victim reported being abducted and held captive on a small boat that was swept away from its mooring during Monday night's storm. She broke out of the boat cabin and swam for shore in the midst of one of the season's worst storms.

"She's lucky to be alive," said Police Chief Grant Hoff. "We are seeking one individual for questioning in the case." He declined to name the individual, who has not been formally charged.

The 17-year-old's parents had always been confident that Alicia would be found.

"Alicia is doing well. She's glad to be back with her family," said her mother, Alice Thorn. Arnold and Alice Thorn live at Bloodwater House, a well-known local landmark, with their two children.

> In an unrelated incident, Arnold Thorn sustained an accidental head injury late yesterday afternoon at his home on Riverview Terrace. He is being treated at Bloodwater Hospital.

Roni let the newspaper fall to her lap and sighed. Why did Brian get all the credit? If it hadn't been for her, he wouldn't even have been there. Plus, he didn't really find Alicia. He more like stumbled over her.

Roni thought back on the events at Bloodwater House. It had surprised her when Alicia had accused Driftwood Doug of kidnapping her. Doug had seemed like a nice guy. Weird, but not evil. Then again, he had run away from the police, so he must be guilty of something.

She had hoped to ask Alicia a few questions, but just then, the police had shown up, including Brian's mother, who was not at all happy to see him back at Bloodwater House. To make matters worse, a few minutes later Mayor Berglund, who never let a photo op pass him by, had shown up with Nick in tow. That was the worst part of it all. Seeing the hurt and angry look on her mother's face. What a lousy way to end an otherwise interesting day.

At least she wasn't in jail. But she might as well be. Nick was working from home, and had been watching her like a cat.

"You can leave your room to go to the bathroom, and for meals," Nick had decreed. "The rest of the time you stay in lockdown. At least until I can look at you without wanting to tear my hair out."

"But . . . there's nothing to do! My computer is dead!"

"And whose fault is that?" The look on Nick's face told Roni not to argue.

She tried to pass the time by rereading some Sherlock Holmes stories, but they weren't as good the second time around. Several times she left her room to attempt to renegotiate the terms of her punishment. Each time her mother ordered her back to her room, refusing to discuss it. Nick was normally pretty easygoing, but this time Roni had pushed her too far. She had not only broken the terms of her grounding, but had spent part of the day hanging out with an accused kidnapper, and then got involved in an unfortunate accident at Bloodwater House.

That was what they were calling it. An unfortunate accident. Lucky for her. Lucky for Brian.

Roni felt awful about letting her mom down. And there were other things she felt awful about—Alicia was back home, living under that same roof with that horrible man. Driftwood Doug, the accused kidnapper, was on the lam. And poor Brian. He had saved her from Mr. Thorn, and found Alicia, and got his name in the paper, and now he was just as grounded as she was.

Worst of all, with everything that had happened over the past couple of days, she had somehow managed to gain three pounds.

The sun coming through the window shone right through Alicia's closed eyes. It was too much work to get up and lower the shade, so she lay there staring at the bloodred insides of her eyelids.

She was tired through to her bones. She might never get up again. If she pretended to be unconscious maybe everyone would leave her alone for the rest of her life. No homework, no arguments, no problems.

She had to stop thinking. She had given them what they wanted. A name. It would keep them busy for a while. Maybe forever. Maybe it would all just go away and she could stay in bed.

She heard footsteps in the hallway. She heard her door creak open. Alicia kept her eyes closed. She felt a cool hand on her forehead, blocking the sun. The hand stroked her hair and she wanted it to never stop.

Her mother leaned down and whispered to her. "I'll never let anyone steal you away from me again. You're safe. Sleep well, my baby."

40

boat puzzle

Brian read the newspaper article over and over again. His name had never been in the paper before. At first, it was exciting, but by the seventh or eighth time he read it the excitement faded. He was still stuck at home, grounded for all of eternity. His mother would never trust him again. Even the fact that he had found Alicia Camden had not deflected his mother's anger.

It was all Roni Delicata's fault. She was the one person who was capable of getting him in worse trouble than he could get himself into.

He wondered how she was doing. He wondered if she was mad at him, since he was getting the credit for finding Alicia. He hoped she wasn't mad. She was scary when she was mad, and not much fun.

He also wondered what had happened to Alicia. Had she really been abducted by Driftwood Doug? If so, why? And if not, then why had Alicia accused him? If it wasn't Doug, then why would she hide the identity of the real kidnapper? Was she protecting someone, or was she just scared?

He had tried to ask his mom about it, but last night she had been in no mood to talk to him, and this morning she had left before he got out of bed. Stuck at home with nothing to do, Brian's brain bounced thoughts from one side of his skull to the other, like a game of mental ping-pong:

Roni Delicata was a bad influence.

Alicia said she was abducted by Driftwood Doug.

It wasn't fair that he was grounded.

He might have saved Roni's life.

It was Roni's fault he was in this mess.

No, it was his own fault.

His mom was completely unreasonable.

Roni was fun.

French donuts and coffee.

Was Driftwood Doug being framed?

A perfect throw!

Mr. Thorn could have been killed.

Where was the boat?

"The boat!" he said aloud, sitting up in bed. He thought hard for several minutes, then swung his feet to the floor and ran downstairs to his father's office.

"Dad, I have a question."

Bruce Bain's head slowly emerged, blinking owlishly, from behind a teetering tower of books.

"You are grounded, young man," he said. Mrs. Bain had coached her husband well.

"I know I'm grounded. That's not the question."

"Oh, I see. What is it, son?".

"Do you still have those Mississippi River charts from when you were working on the clam book?"

"Ah yes, *Bivalves of the Upper Mississippi*. One of my most successful research papers. You want the maps?" Bruce Bain stroked his long chin. "I believe they are near my flatworm photographs." He went directly to a stack of mismatched files piled six feet high, grabbed a manila file folder from the middle of the stack, and pulled it out. The stack teetered, but somehow did not fall.

"There you are, son. What are you working on?"

"School project," said Brian, giving his standard answer.

"Good, good! Well, keep up the good work, son!"

Brian went back to his room and sorted through the maps until he found the one showing the section of river just south of Bloodwater. The map had been designed for barge operators and boaters. It showed all the islands, sandbars, channels, and backwaters.

The boat was the key. The police might look for it, sure, but not very hard. Brian knew how cops' brains worked. When his mom decided he was guilty of something, that was it. Excuses, explanations, evidence, reasonable doubt . . . none of that meant a thing.

Of course, she was almost always right.

Maybe the cops were right about Driftwood Doug. They had Alicia's word that he had kidnapped her. And Doug had fled, which was very suspicious.

Brian spread the map out on the floor. Alicia said she had been held prisoner on a boat, and that the boat had been swept away in the storm. So where was the boat?

He put his finger on Wolf Spider Island, where Alicia said the boat had been tied up. He imagined a boat cast loose in a storm. He would have to calculate the wind direction and wind speed. And the water level during the storm. It was a puzzle. A boat puzzle.

Brian bent over the map.

He liked puzzles.

41

closet cleaning

Sitting at her desk, doodling on the back of her notebook, Roni wondered if maybe this time she had actually learned her lesson. She shouldn't meddle in things. Maybe it was time for her to focus on getting better grades in her classes so she could go to a good college and get a job at the *Washington Post* and win a Pulitzer Prize.

She blinked and her so-called wonderful life disappeared. She looked at what she had been doodling. A boat. The boat. Alicia had told Brian she'd been held prisoner on a boat. A boat that had been tied up at Wolf Spider Island.

What boat?

Driftwood Doug's boat? How many boats did Driftwood Doug have?

Roni thought back to Bloodwater House. She had looked into Arnold Thorn's eyes. She was sure he was hiding something. Could Alicia be lying to protect him? Arnold Thorn had once owned a boat, but according to Ted it had been vandalized and sold. Sold to who? Or had Arnold Thorn hidden it away someplace—like maybe Wolf Spider Island. She imagined Alicia locked inside, made a prisoner by her own stepfather.

Roni started digging through her old files. The phone number she needed had to be in there someplace.

After a few minutes she found a file labeled "Wolf Spider Island."

Now she needed a phone. Roni pushed open her bedroom door and listened. Nick was in the kitchen talking on the house phone, working out last-minute details for the Bloodwater Apple Festival. Roni sneaked down the stairs, keeping her feet toward the edge of the steps to avoid squeaking. Nick's purse hung from the coat rack in the front hall. Roni reached the purse without being detected, grabbed her mom's cell phone, and tiptoed back upstairs to her room.

Nick was still talking. Grabbing her pillow off the bed, Roni backed into her closet and pulled the door closed behind her. She jammed the pillow into the crack under the door and punched in the phone number.

Sitting in the dark with the phone right next to her face, she felt as if she were in a thriller movie. The escaped convict psychopathic chain saw killer was in the next room. This phone call was her only hope.

On the fourth ring, a man's deep voice answered, saying, "No, I don't want to buy no aluminum siding."

"Hoot?" she whispered.

"Who is this? What are you selling?"

"It's me. Roni."

"I don't want any!"

"Roni Delicata!" she whispered more loudly.

"Oh. The burglar. You the one sent the gestapo after poor old Doug?"

"No! That's what I'm calling about. Hoot, how many boats does Doug have?"

"Boats? Well, he's got his houseboat. And he's got that canoe, if you call that a boat."

"Is that all?"

"How many boats does a guy need?"

"I don't know. Have there been any new boats docked around the island the last month or so?"

"Well . . . Candle Andy got himself a kayak. And there was an old cabin cruiser tied up at the north end last few weeks. Don't know whose that was. It's gone now. Mighta got blowed off in the storm."

Roni felt her heart speed up. "Hoot, remember a couple of years ago when that big wind came through and tore a bunch of boats loose from their docks?"

"Do I remember? I lost my dinghy that night!"

"You ever find it?"

"Sure did. Ended up way down in Alma, a good thirty miles. 'Course, the water was really high that year. Not like now."

"If a boat was lost in the storm we had last night, where do you suppose it would wash up?"

"Hmm," Hoot said. Roni pictured him rubbing his chin. "My guess is she'd hang up at Nun's Island."

"The island down by the convent?"

"Yeah. Big old sandbar hanging off the end of the island. Catches lots of driftwood and junk. Even after that storm we had the water's still pretty low. You could probably wade out there. If you don't mind leeches."

"Roni!" Nick hollered from out in the hall.

"Thanks. Gotta go." Roni turned off the cell phone, shoved it in her pocket, and tumbled out of her closet just as her mom pushed open the door.

"What are you doing?" her mother asked. She was dressed for work, her purse hanging over her shoulder.

"I thought I'd take advantage of my incarceration by cleaning my closet."

"You haven't gotten very far."

"I'm working out a plan."

Nick raised her eyebrows in disbelief, then shrugged, apparently deciding that pretending to believe her daughter was easier than getting into a confusing argument. "I have to go down to city hall for a few hours. I assume I don't need to tell you that you are to stay here."

"I'm going to be very busy with the closet. I don't see how I could possibly leave."

Her mom stuck her head in Roni's closet. Roni took the opportunity to slip the cell phone back into her mother's purse.

Nick emerged, saying, "You've got some work ahead of you."

Roni thought of her latest plan. "I think you're right."

As soon as the door closed behind her mother, Roni dove back into the closet, this time searching for a pair of leech-proof tights.

151

42

imelda

"Brian?" Bruce Bain peered in through the doorway to Brian's room.

"Hey, Dad," Brian said. He had been checking his e-mail for the umpteenth time. Lots of spam. No Roni.

Mr. Bain stepped over a terrarium containing several small amphibians, waded through a morass of slightly smelly clothes, detoured around a nest of computer cables and partially disassembled peripheral devices, and looked down at the river map spread across Brian's unmade bed.

"How is your research going?"

"Good. I've been trying to figure out where a boat might end up if it got torn loose in that storm we had."

Brian's father leaned over the map. "Show me."

Brian had placed several chess pieces where he thought a small boat might have been docked, and at spots along the river where it might have run aground.

"What is the likely point of origin?" his father asked.

"Wolf Spider Island," said Brian, touching the black queen.

"How large a boat?"

"Probably not very big." Brian moved his finger down the map. "Assuming that the boat was set adrift here . . ." He moved his finger downstream to the white bishop. "There is a sandbar here at Point No Point." He moved his finger again, to the black rook. "And here we have this small island." He moved his finger again. "Or it might have gone all the way to the lock and dam at Alma."

"Which would you say is most probable?" Mr. Bain asked.

Brian stabbed his finger at the black rook. "The island."

"I agree. I would give that a probability of somewhat over 80 percent." Mr. Bain frowned. "Why did you want to know all this, son?"

"Just curious."

"Oh." That was good enough for Mr. Bain, who spent his life in pursuit of obscure, pointless facts.

As far as Roni knew, no nuns lived on Nun's Island. It got its name because it was just offshore from the convent, eight miles south of Bloodwater.

Eight miles was a long way to walk. And she only had about four hours before Nick returned home. She picked up the house phone and called Brian. The phone rang about eight times before she gave up. She was on her own.

Minutes later, Roni was riding through downtown Bloodwater on Imelda, her ancient Huffy Princess with the pink frame, pink tires, and a pink vinyl seat. She had left her trenchcoat at home, replacing it with a black leather jacket that was a size too small. A fluorescent orange helmet and an enormous pair of sunglasses completed her outfit.

She prayed no one she knew would see her. At least she'd had the good sense to scrape the Mary-Kate and Ashley sticker off her bike.

Making a wide detour around city hall—it would not be good to run into Nick—she made her way through town to the highway and followed it south. By the time she passed the turnoff to Wolf Spider Island her legs were throbbing and her butt was numb. Oh well, she thought, maybe I'll lose that three pounds.

"You actually saw one? A Migglebruster Spattertail?"

"I *think* it was a Spattertail," Brian said. "It *looked* like a Spattertail."

"That would be very strange indeed," said Mr. Nestor.

They were a few miles south of Bloodwater on Highway 61, driving past the turnoff to Wolf Spider Island.

"A Migglebruster Spattertail . . . at this time of year! So far north! Remarkable! And you saw it where?"

"Just down the road a few miles. By the convent." Brian felt terrible about lying to poor Mr. Nestor, but he hadn't been able to think of another way to get to Nun's Island. What he *should* have done was to call his mom and tell her what he suspected. Why hadn't he done that? Brian didn't want to think too hard about that question. He knew the answer. He wanted to be the one to solve the case. Roni Delicata had infected him with the investigative reporter virus.

"My goodness! Some young people certainly do dress oddly!" said Mr. Nestor.

Brian looked out the window. A bicyclist wearing a bright orange helmet, oversize sunglasses, a black leather jacket, black sneakers, and blue tights was hunched over the handlebars of a pink-tired pink bicycle, pedaling furiously.

Almost there. Pedal a hundred more times, Roni told herself, then coast for a while. One, two, three, four . . .

A dark green Jeep went flying past. That wasn't so bad. It was the semis that really scared her. Roni kept counting: twenty-six, twenty-seven, twenty-eight . . .

It was the tenth time she had forced herself through the one-hundred-pedal routine. It helped to have little goals with a promised rest at the end. She was getting closer, almost halfway to one hundred—forty-seven, forty-eight, forty-nine—

BLAM!

Roni's heart shot into her throat as Imelda skidded to the left. She corrected just in time, braked to a stop, then jumped off and stared forlornly at the shredded remains of her back tire.

43

sister louise

Mr. Nestor, happily running and jumping through a field of goldenrod, had already forgotten Brian's existence. Brian turned toward the river and considered his options.

The easiest way to get to Nun's Island would be to walk down the long driveway past the convent. But Brian didn't want to get too close to the nuns. He wouldn't know what to say if he ran into one.

He decided to cut straight through the woods to the river. He waded into the weeds at the side of the road and plunged into the woods. Arriving at the water's edge with only a few scratches, he looked up and down the river.

Nun's Island was visible a few hundred yards downstream.

He made his way along the shore, weaving through thickets of river willow, climbing over tangles of dead trees, and crashing through stands of purple loosestrife. He soon had a clear view of the island. His calculations had proven correct—the island was a trap for floating objects: fallen trees, driftwood, scrap lumber, soda bottles, and plastic bags. And there, at the far end of the island, was something that looked like a small cabin cruiser, jouncing and bobbing in the waves.

Roni pulled some dead branches over Imelda to hide her— then wondered why she bothered. Who would want her?

Walking was easier on the butt than riding the bike, but she was still a mile from Nun's Island. After walking for twenty minutes, Roni revised her estimate—maybe it was more like two miles. Or three. And her tights were starting to bind. This was not good.

Roni was thinking dark, self-pitying thoughts when a white minivan pulled over to the shoulder. A young woman stuck her head out the window.

"Do you need a lift?"

Looking at the woman's smiling, open face, Roni decided to risk being abducted. She ran to the passenger door and jumped in.

"Where're you going?" the woman asked.

"The convent," Roni told her as they pulled back onto the highway.

"Oh, are you a communicant?"

"Um, I don't think so." Whatever a communicant was, Roni was pretty sure she wasn't one.

The young woman laughed. "I didn't introduce myself. I'm Sister Louise."

"You're a nun?"

"Yes, I'm a nun."

"You don't look like a nun."

"I'm in mufti."

"What's mufti?"

"It means I'm out of uniform."

"Oh." Roni took a closer look at the nun's clothing: long flowered skirt, white blouse, and clunky shoes. Not exactly a fashion plate. "They let you wear anything you want?"

"Within reason. Of course, we don't often dress as, er, creatively as you young people." She gave Roni's blue tights and black leather jacket a sideways look.

"I know, I look like a clown. You should've seen me when I had my helmet on. But I always thought those head things you wear were kinda cool."

"Our wimples? Actually, they're kind of hot. I mean literally hot." The nun-in-mufti laughed at her own joke. "Why are you going to the convent?" she asked.

"Looking for something."

The sister nodded and turned off the road down a long driveway. "Most people who come here are looking for something."

"I mean I'm *literally* looking for something. A boat."

"A boat?"

"A boat that got away," Roni said.

44

the cap'n arnold

Nun's Island rose out of the water less than forty feet from the shore. It looked easy to wade out to, but the underwater boulders were slick and hard to see in the silty river water. Brian slipped and fell twice on the way there, completely drenching himself before he got to shore.

The island was only about three hundred yards long and a hundred yards wide, but it took Brian nearly half an hour to pick his way through the prickly, poisonous underbrush. He reached the far end and found the boat, a small cabin cruiser, only about twenty-five feet long. The prow had ridden up onto a half-submerged log; the stern was bobbing low in the water.

There was ten feet of water between Brian and the boat. He would have to get wet again. Brian looked down at himself and shrugged. He couldn't get any wetter, that was for sure.

He stepped into the water. His feet sank ankle deep into ooze. He half slogged, half swam through the water and grabbed the gunwale near the stern. Lifting one leg over the gunwale, he hoisted himself up. He did an unintentional somersault into the boat, cracking his elbow on the deck. After checking himself over for broken bones, he stood and looked around.

The boat was old, with lots of wood and nice detailing, but it was in terrible condition. Several inches of water pooled on the floor. The vinyl captain's chair was slashed open, and the control panel looked as though someone had taken a hammer to it.

Ted Thorn had said his stepdad's boat had been vandalized. This could be it.

A small door, slightly ajar, led to the area under the front half of the boat. Brian peeked inside. There was more water sloshing around, and a strange smell, like bilgewater mixed with perfume.

He pushed the door all the way open, ducked his head, and went in.

Sometimes things just worked out. Sister Louise insisted on giving Roni a ride out to the island in a small rowboat.

"No point in getting your remarkable outfit all wet." Sister Louise laughed. She laughed a lot. Roni hadn't known that nuns laughed *ever*.

"Well . . . thanks."

"We saw that boat out there after the storm," Sister Louise said as she used an oar to push the rowboat away from the dock. "We called the marina in Bloodwater, but they said nobody there was missing a boat. Is it yours?"

"No. But I think I know the owner." She had decided not to tell Sister Louise what she suspected about the boat. Roni wanted to solve this mystery on her own.

"There it is," said the sister.

As they approached the cruiser, Roni made out two words in script on the back of the boat: *Cap'n Arnold*.

"That's the one," Roni said. It was obviously Arnold Thorn's craft. What a story this would make.

Sister Louise asked, "How long do you think you'll be? I have afternoon prayers in about twenty minutes."

"I might be a while," Roni said. She liked Sister Louise, but she didn't want her looking over her shoulder as she investigated. "I'll be okay on my own."

"Are you sure? How about if I come back for you in an hour or so?"

"That would be great," Roni said. "Thank you."

She grabbed the small ladder attached to the back of the boat and climbed on board, then watched as Sister Louise rowed back toward shore. Standing alone on the swaying, creaking old boat, Roni suddenly felt very vulnerable.

Brian, ankle deep in bilgewater, looked around the cramped sleeping quarters. He wasn't sure what he was looking for, but he quickly figured out where the weird smell was coming from—a big bunch of flowers rotting in a tipped-over vase. Faint voices drifted in from outside. He heard a thump, and the back of the boat sank a few inches. His heart began to pound. Someone had climbed aboard. But who? Arnold Thorn?

He tried to think. Worst-case scenario—it was the culprit returning to the scene of the crime. Worse-than-worst-case scenario—it was his mother.

He looked frantically around the small cabin. No place to hide. He flattened himself against the bulkhead. Maybe whoever it was would just glance into the cabin and not notice him.

The door to the cabin opened. Brian held his breath.

"Yoo-hoo!"

He knew that voice. He let his breath out quietly and grinned. Some crazy girl with a notebook and a phony nose ring was about to get the scare of her life.

"Any ghosts down there? Any dead bodies?"

It was all Brian could do not to laugh.

"Any rats? Any snakes? You better hide, 'cause here I come!"

He heard her footsteps, then saw her black sneakers and blue tights and suddenly realized that the oddly dressed girl on the pink bicycle had been Roni. Again, he had to fight down laughter.

He waited until one millisecond before she would have seen him, then shouted, "Rat snakes!"

It was better than he could have imagined.

Roni let out an eardrum-shattering squeal. Her feet flew out from under her and she skidded down the last two steps, landing on her butt in the bilgewater.

A laugh burst out of Brian, but when he saw the look on Roni's face he clamped his hand over his mouth. He hadn't taken two things into account.

Number one, Roni was quick to recover.

Number two, Roni was quick to anger.

Brian backed up as fast and as far as he could in the cramped cabin. Roni came after him like an angry mother cat.

"Wait! It's just me!" But Roni already had him by the shoulders and was bouncing him off the wall.

"I"—*thud*—"know"—*thud*—"it's"—*thud*—"you!"

Suddenly she stopped shoving him. Brian stared at her face. It was not a nice face at all. Gasping for breath, with her hair all wet and straggly and the black leather jacket and tights and the ferocious scowl, she looked like a crazy killer bimbo from some ultraviolent comic book. He hoped she wouldn't start hitting him. In a situation like this there was only one thing to do.

"I'm sorry," he said.

rotting roses

"Are you mad because you didn't get here first?" Brian asked.

Roni gave him the meanest look she could muster. He *so* didn't get it. She said, "No, Stink Bomb, I'm mad at you because you're an immature jerkball."

They were on the upper deck, sitting on opposite sides of the boat, trying to dry off. Roni had hung her leather jacket over the starboard running light. Brian took off his mud-filled shoes and rinsed them in the river.

"I said I was sorry."

"I don't like being scared like that."

"Yeah, well, I don't like getting shoved around. Especially by a girl."

"What's that supposed to mean?"

"Nothing."

Roni decided to ignore the little twerp. About thirty seconds passed. It was a long time for Roni to go without talking, but she was really, really mad.

"Anyway," said Brian, "we found it."

Roni shrugged. She *was* a bit miffed that Brian had beat her to it. First he beats her to Alicia, now this. Not that a few minutes' difference mattered. They were partners. Or they used to be, before the stupid freshman pulled his "rat snakes" bit. She shuddered.

"What do we do now?" Brian asked. "Call the police? Call the FBI? Call the Army Reserve? Call waiting?"

Roni tried and failed to control the smirk that jumped to her lips, but she quickly squelched it and continued to ignore him. After a few seconds Brian got up and went back down to the sleeping cabin.

"I think we might have contaminated a crime scene," he shouted up from the doorway.

Roni couldn't resist. "And whose fault was that?"

Brian was looking carefully at the door. "The door's been kicked open."

"Well, duh!"

"Did you notice that smell? It's coming from a bunch of rotten flowers in a vase."

"Flowers?" Roni was still mad at him, but this was business. She went to the top of the steps and looked down. Brian picked something up and held it up to her. The blossom was a soggy mess, but the thorny stem was enough to identify it as a rose.

"I wonder if this was from Maurice," Brian said.

Roni knew she should go down and have a look around, but she was still too freaked out by the thought of rats and snakes. Especially the rats. She had this thing about naked-tailed rodents.

"Did you find anything else?"

"No. Wait, there's something jammed under the bed. Got it!" Brian handed up a soggy green bundle. Roni dragged it out into the light. She recognized it right away. Just forty-eight hours earlier Alicia Camden had whacked her with this very same lime green designer backpack.

"Think we should open it?" Brian asked.

"Probably not." Roni unzipped the pack. "Contamination of evidence and all." She dumped the contents onto the deck.

"Good technique," Brian said, watching Roni paw through Alicia's possessions. Three tubes of lipstick with names like Tawny Puce, Orange Crush, and Deadly Red. Hair accessories of every sort: clips, scrunchies, barrettes. A comb and a brush. A few schoolbooks, a *Cosmopolitan* magazine, and a copy of the *Bloodwater Pump*. Everything was soaked.

Roni unzipped one of the side pockets and pulled out a small notebook, also wet and swollen. It looked like a kind of diary or daybook. Roni carefully peeled apart the sodden pages. Unfortunately, Alicia had used a purple felt-tip pen for most of her entries. Much of the writing was too smeared and blurry to read, but a few entries written in black ink had survived.

"Listen to this," Roni said. *"Breakfast: One half grapefruit, three tablespoons yogurt, one cup herbal tea.* Sounds like a recipe for starvation. No wonder she's so skinny."

"See if you can read her last entries," Brian suggested.

"I'm trying." The wet pages were hard to separate without tearing them. "Here we go . . . this looks like last Friday." Roni looked at Brian. "That was the day she got beat up. It says, *Seeing Maurice tonight. We are getting so close. He brought me roses yesterday—a whole dozen! I just wish he wasn't so jealous. Sometimes I'm afraid. He threatened to . . .*" Roni looked up. "I can't read the rest of it." She looked down into the cabin where the vase of rotting roses lay. "Maybe it was Maurice after all."

"Yeah, but Mr. Thorn attacked you," Brian reminded her. "And this is his boat."

"He didn't actually *attack* me," Roni said. "He just sort of grabbed me. He wanted to see what I was writing in my notebook."

"He pushed you into the pool," Brian reminded her.

"Well . . . actually, I was sort of falling anyway, and he grabbed me, and then I kicked him and fell in."

"You mean . . . I almost killed him and he wasn't doing anything wrong?"

"I'm not sure. He might have been about to do something."

"Don't forget that Driftwood Doug saw Mr. Thorn standing over Alicia that night."

"Yes, but he also said he saw a tall man running away through the woods. That could have been Maurice."

Brian nodded. "What else does it say? Turn the page."

Roni peeled back the next wet page. There was one more entry.

"It says, *I hate him I hate him I hate him I hate him!*"

"Is she talking about Maurice or her stepdad?"

"Who knows? For all we know she was talking about Mickey Mouse."

"Nobody hates Mickey Mouse," Brian said.

"I do."

Brian gave her a shocked look.

"He's a *rodent*," Roni said.

the three dwarfs

Riding in a boat was much nicer than wading through muddy water, Brian decided. Sister Louise tied the boat to the dock below the convent as Roni and Brian hopped out.

"Thanks, Sister," said Roni.

"Yeah, thanks a lot," said Brian.

"You are both welcome. I can give you a ride back to town, but not until Sister Mary brings the van back. It might be a couple of hours."

"That's okay," said Roni. "We'll walk."

Brian did not like hearing that. He was exhausted and wet, his arms were covered with scratches, and his shoes made grunting sounds with every soggy step. He felt like he was carrying ten gallons of water in his clothes. Jeans could suck up several times their weight in water. That would be an interesting experiment. He'd have to try it sometime.

"Now what?" he asked as they reached the highway. He looked at Roni. She wasn't looking her best. He had to laugh.

"What's so funny?" she asked.

"You look like the three dwarfs."

She gave him that look—the one she had given him on the bench outside of Spindler's office, like she couldn't decide whether to laugh or punch him in the nose. "Okay, I'll bite. What are you talking about?"

"The three dwarfs," Brian said. "Soggy, Muddy, and Droopy."

"Very funny."

"I do my best."

"Okay, smart guy, where do you think we go from here?"

"Home. Get into some dry clothes."

Roni was giving him the look again.

"What?" he said.

"Don't you want to know what really happened to Alicia?"

"Sure, but, I mean . . . look at us! Soggy, Muddy, Droopy, and Soaked. Not to mention Hungry."

"That's not important. We have to talk to Maurice. He should be home from school by now."

"Why Maurice?"

"He's the one who gave her the roses."

Brian frowned. "I think we should try to see Alicia. She's the one with the answers."

"We'd never get past her mother."

"We could send a note in with Ted. Tell her we found her backpack. That might get her to talk to us."

"That's a good idea . . ." Roni started walking, trailing her jacket and Alicia's backpack. "But my idea's better. I say we start with Maurice. You coming or not?"

"Okay, but how do we get there?"

Roni stuck out her thumb.

The pickup truck was an old, faded-red Ford. The doors were painted with the words KATO SIGN CO. and a phone number. A man with tousled reddish hair rolled down the window and looked them over.

"Need a lift?" he asked.

"We're going into Bloodwater," Roni said.

"You willing to get in a truck with a stranger?"

"My mom's a cop," Brian said. He figured it couldn't hurt to let the guy know.

The man laughed. "Hop in then."

Roni and Brian climbed into the back of the truck.

"You can sit up front," the guy said, sticking his head out the window and looking back at them.

"No, we're too grungy."

"Don't matter to this old mule."

"That's okay," Roni said. "We like riding in back."

"Suit yourself."

He put the truck in gear and pulled back onto the highway. Wind whistled through their clothes. They were wet and cold. Empty paint cans rattled around the truckbed.

"I'm freezing," Brian said through clenched teeth.

"Yeah," Roni said.

"I promised my mom I would never, ever hitchhike."

"Me, too," Roni said.

"I wrecked my shoes."

Roni looked down at his shoes. They did indeed look wrecked.

"Whose idea was this anyway?" Brian asked.

Roni didn't say anything. She looked down at her clothes. They were drying out a bit, but she was not exactly presentable. She didn't really want to see Maurice like this. A girl's got her pride, even in front of a possible kidnapper. But she didn't want to wait, either. They were so close to solving the mystery she could taste it.

The pickup truck driver dropped them off in downtown Bloodwater.

"I've got two kids about your age," he told them. "If I ever caught them hitchhiking, I'd have something to say about it. Well, you be good now." The guy waved as he pulled away.

Roni walked up to the windows of the Hallmark store and tried to get a glimpse of herself. Her hair was mostly dry, her jacket covered most of her wet clothes, and, after she pulled up her bagging tights, she didn't look so bad.

"You're a doll," Brian told her, standing next to her, looking like a twit. "A rag doll." He laughed.

"Hey," he said as she walked away. Roni resolved to not talk to him all the way to Maurice's house.

"There was something I noticed in the boat—" he said, but she kept walking. "Don't you want to know what I figured out?" he asked.

"No. Just shut up for a while." Roni was sick of listening to his juvenile jokes. She kept walking.

He fell into step beside her and they walked the five blocks to Maurice's with only the sound of Brian's wet shoes grunting.

47

floating islands

A little voice in Alicia's head kept asking questions. Questions like water pounding against the hull of a boat. Pounding and pounding. She felt as if she were drowning all over again, only this time in her own lies.

Would anyone ever believe her again?

It's all going to come out, Alicia thought. Every crummy little detail. And then everything will fall apart. It'll be the end.

She could hear her mom on the phone, her voice carrying all the way up the curving marble staircase and under the door of Alicia's bedroom. It was a huge house, but not huge enough for them to get away from each other.

Alicia knew exactly what her mother was wearing—the new Anne Klein teal blue sweater with the too-tight Ralph Lauren jeans and Cole Haan heels. She could almost always guess which look she'd go with on any given day. It made it easier for Alicia to pick out her own outfit. Her mother liked them to look like twin sisters. Alicia knew it was weird, but she usually went along with it anyway. It was her mom's idea of being close.

Alicia would have preferred a hug. But hugs for kids were in short supply at Bloodwater House. Even when Alicia made it home after that awful night on the boat, her mom hadn't really hugged her. They were like floating islands on an icy ocean, swirling around each other, colliding occasionally but never gently touching.

Her mother would be leaving soon to pick up Arnold at the hospital. Alicia wished her mom had never met Arnold Thorn, had never moved here to Bloodwater House. They could still be living in their little two-bedroom house in Mankato with her real dad, the only home she'd known for her first fifteen years. Maybe her dad wasn't rich, but he had loved her. He had kept her safe. Back then her brother Ted had been a cute little hellion, always dirty and full of wild grins and mischief. Now he was turning into a mini Arnold.

Her mom had wanted money and prestige. A big house. Nice clothes. But now that she had all that, she still wasn't happy.

Alicia stared out her window across the pool and tennis court into the woods. Already the maples were sporting a bright gold and orange fringe. Summer was long gone. In a month or two everything would be white and frozen.

It doesn't matter anymore, she told herself. By the time they get back from the hospital I'll be long gone.

48

dead fish

"Let me do the talking," Roni said.

"Whatever," said Brian. The ride in the pickup had almost dried him off, but his jeans remained uncomfortably wet in the crotch, and his shoes were still making weird noises.

Maurice was in his driveway cleaning the wheels of his Ford Explorer. He looked up as Roni and Brian approached.

"You come to blackmail me some more?" he said.

"Just a few questions," said Roni.

Maurice glared at her, shook his head, and went back to cleaning a glob of tar off one of the wheel covers.

Roni said, "You told me you were in class Monday afternoon when Alicia was abducted."

"So?" Maurice dipped his rag in a jar of cleaning compound and rubbed furiously at the tar.

Roni said, "But you were late for basketball practice. Why was that?"

Maurice stopped scrubbing and looked up at them. "What do you want from me?"

"The truth," said Roni.

Maurice shook his head, stood up, and threw down the rag.

"Look, I didn't do anything wrong, okay?"

"Where were you Monday afternoon?"

"I went to see Alicia, okay? I went over to her house to try to talk to her. Nobody was home."

"What time was that?"

"About one-thirty. So I went for a drive and lost track of time and got to practice late. End of story."

"When was the last time you gave Alicia roses?" Roni asked.

Maurice looked startled. "Last Thursday. Why?"

"Where were you?"

Maurice shook his head slowly, as if reluctant to revisit the memory. "Look, Alicia's home, okay? It's over. Why are you being such a pain?"

"It's what I do," said Roni.

"If you want to know what happened to Alicia, ask Alicia. Now go away." Maurice returned his attention to polishing his wheels.

Brian, who had not spoken the entire time, said, "How about giving us a lift over to Bloodwater House?"

"The munchkin speaks," said Maurice, not looking up. "Why should I do you any favors?"

"Because we know where your boat is," Brian said.

Maurice stared at Brian with his mouth hanging open. "Where?" he asked, standing up.

"Not where you left it," Brian said.

"I know that. It blew away in the storm. Where is it?" He stepped toward Brian, towering over him.

"Give us a ride to Alicia's and I'll tell you."

"You'll tell me now, you little twerp."

Roni looked from one to the other. Maurice's boat? How was the *Cap'n Arnold* Maurice's boat? Maurice was getting red in the face, never a good sign.

"I'll tell you after we talk to Alicia," Brian said.

Maurice's hands closed into fists and his mouth got very small and tight.

"I paid five hundred dollars for that boat."

"You bought it from Arnold Thorn?" Roni asked.

Maurice nodded. "He gave me a deal on it. After it got vandalized."

"Vandalized by who?" Roni asked, thinking of the way Maurice had keyed Tyrone's car.

Maurice shrugged, looking away.

Roni thought: Aha! Maurice vandalizes the Thorns' boat, then buys it for cheap, then he beats up his girlfriend, then he locks her away in his boat. Case closed?

Something wasn't right. Why would Alicia keep it a secret? Why would she accuse Driftwood Doug? Why had Arnold Thorn tried to grab her notebook away from her, and what was he afraid of?

Brian said, "How about that ride, Maurice?"

Before he would let them in his car, Maurice went inside to get something to cover the seats. "No offense, but you two look kinda soggy," he said.

As soon as he was out of hearing, Roni turned to Brian. "How did you know it was his boat?"

"It was just a wild guess. Ted told us that his stepdad had sold the boat, so I thought maybe Maurice had bought it."

Maurice came out of the house with an armload of newspapers and spread them over the seats in his SUV.

"Okay, soggy bottoms, hop in."

The papers crinkled as they sat on them, Roni in the front seat and Brian in back. No one said much during the drive to Bloodwater House. They couldn't. Maurice had cranked the tunes up super loud to show off the subwoofers he had installed under the seats. It was like getting a butt massage. Roni looked back at Brian. He was waving his arms around like a singer in a hip-hop video. She winked at him. He stared back at her. Maybe he couldn't wink.

Maurice drove the same way he ran around the basketball court: fast, with lots of sharp turns. Brian was trying to be cool in the backseat, working his arm routine to the music, when he noticed Roni's eye twitching. Maybe she was trying to wink, but it looked too spasmodic for that. She looked a mess. It must be hard for a girl to be wet and grubby. Girls just couldn't pull off the mud-stained look as good as a guy.

Maurice said something.

"What?" Brian yelled.

"I said, 'You guys smell like dead fish!' "

Brian looked at Roni. Her eyes had narrowed to tiny slits. He hoped she wouldn't do anything to Maurice while the SUV was moving.

They made it to Bloodwater House without incident.

Maurice pulled over to the curb opposite the front gate, across the street from an old pickup truck. He cut the music.

Roni and Brian both stared at the pickup, faded red with KATO SIGN CO. painted on the side.

"Roni said, "Hey . . . isn't that the truck . . ."

"It sure is," said Brian.

"What are you talking about?" Maurice asked.

The front gate swung open and a man with tousled reddish hair came out carrying a bag in one hand, pulling Alicia toward the pickup truck with the other.

Maurice jumped out of the Explorer. "Alicia!" he shouted.

The red-haired man threw the bag in back, opened the door of the pickup, and pushed Alicia into the passenger seat.

Roni was already out the door and running toward them. She had almost reached the truck when it suddenly lurched forward. Roni yelled, but the driver kept going, accelerating quickly.

Alicia looked back at them, wide-eyed, through the rear window.

crash

Brian, still sitting in the backseat, was confused. He thought he'd figured everything out, but now Alicia was being carried off by the pickup truck guy. What was going on?

Roni ran back toward the Explorer. Maurice stood uncertainly on the sidewalk, watching the pickup racing away.

"Follow them!" Roni shouted at Maurice.

"Why?" Maurice asked. "If she wants to go off with some other guy, that's her business."

Roni didn't bother to argue. She pushed past Maurice, jumped into the driver's seat, and punched the accelerator to the floor, leaving Maurice standing in a cloud of burnt rubber.

"What are you doing?" Brian said.

"Going after them, what do you think?" said Roni. She was leaning over the steering wheel, her jaw clenched.

"I think you're out of your mind."

"You know who that is, don't you?" They were gaining rapidly on the old pickup.

"Yeah, that same guy that picked us up hitchhiking—but what do we do if we catch him?"

Roni started honking the horn. The driver of the pickup looked back at them, then sped up. Roni stomped on the gas and stayed close on their tail—way too close, in Brian's opinion. They were coming up on the intersection with Highway 61 when a silver SUV turned onto Riverview, cutting across both lanes. The pickup swerved to avoid a collision, hit the curb, and spun out of control, taking out a mailbox and ending up sideways on the street.

Roni slammed on the brakes. The wheels locked and the Explorer skidded toward the back end of the truck.

What Roni found most surprising about her first car accident was the way everything slowed down. She knew the moment she saw the pickup truck skid sideways that they were going to hit it. She opened her mouth to share that bit of information with Brian, but for some reason her vocal cords weren't working. Then it occurred to her that she hadn't fastened her seat belt. Too late now, she thought as, in slow motion, the nose of the Explorer smashed into the side of the pickup truck box and the air bag exploded in her face with a loud *bang*.

Brian found himself facedown on the floor between the seats. It took him a few seconds to make sure he wasn't broken. His arms and legs seemed to work fine. He climbed back onto the seat. The cab was hazy with white dust from the exploded air bag. Roni was sitting behind the wheel with a shocked look on her face.

"Are you okay?" Brian asked.

"I think so." She was covered with white powder from the air bag.

"We'd better get out of here," he said. "In case it blows up or something."

"That only happens in the movies."

"You sure about that?"

"No."

Brian opened his door and hopped out of the Explorer.

Roni's door was jammed shut. She had to climb over the seat and follow Brian out the back door. As she stepped out of the Explorer, she felt a hand grasp her by the elbow to steady her. For a moment she thought it was Brian, and was surprised by his thoughtfulness. Then she saw who the hand belonged to.

"Let me go!" she shouted, trying to yank her arm from his grasp.

The red-haired man held on tight. "Calm down," he said. He grabbed her by both shoulders. "Are you all right? Do you want to sit down?"

"No!" Roni twisted out of the man's grasp and backed away, looking around frantically. Brian stood helplessly a few feet away, just watching.

"Those air bags are like a punch in the face," said the man. He gave her a lopsided smile. "But they're a lot softer than the windshield."

Roni looked past the man and saw Alicia standing right behind him, and suddenly she understood. "I know who you are," she said.

50

red nails

The silver SUV that caused the accident had pulled over a half block up the street. A man and a woman got out. Brian glanced at them, then did a double take. The woman was running toward them. The man followed her, only more slowly. It was Mr. and Mrs. Thorn. Mr. Thorn's forehead was covered with a large white bandage.

The redheaded man saw the Thorns coming and seemed to deflate.

"I'm sorry, honey," he said to Alicia.

Alicia looked completely shattered. She backed up against the crumpled box of the pickup truck and hid her face behind her hands. The redheaded man wrapped his arms around her and looked defiantly at Mrs. Thorn as she ran up to them, her face red with anger.

"I should have known it was you, you pathetic worm!"

Brian edged over toward Roni. He heard a siren in the distance.

"Now, Alice," said the man. "Let's all calm down. You know how you get."

"How I get? You kidnap my daughter and you want me to calm down?"

The sound got louder. A police cruiser turned off the highway, siren howling, wheels skittering on the asphalt, and stopped with a whoop of its siren. Two cops jumped out—Garth Spall, with his hand on his gun, and a woman in plain-clothes: Brian's mom.

Brian noticed a third person in the police cruiser—a thin, clean-shaven man with a crewcut.

Mrs. Thorn pointed a red-nailed finger at the man holding Alicia.

"That's my ex-husband, Bill Camden," said Mrs. Thorn. "He kidnapped my daughter. Arrest him!"

It was like a really bad movie, only it was happening all around her, and she was in it. Alicia squeezed her eyes closed, but she couldn't close her ears.

"Arrest me for what?" her father asked.

"For kidnapping my daughter," her mother shouted.

"She's my daughter, too," her dad said.

She was just a thing for them to fight over. A daughter thing. She opened her eyes and saw Arnold hovering in the background with that big white bandage on his head.

The policewoman stepped in and raised her voice. "Now, people, I want everybody to CALM DOWN!"

For a few seconds, nobody said a word.

"Thank you," said the policewoman. "Now, Mr. Camden, would you please step away from Alicia?"

Camden released Alicia and took a step to the side. "I didn't kidnap anybody," he said. "She called and asked me to come and get her. Ask her if you don't believe me."

Alicia hugged herself. Even after the divorce they were still fighting. She was nothing more than a game piece.

"Is that true, Alicia?" asked the policewoman.

Alicia thought furiously. She looked at her father, then she looked past her father and saw Maurice Wellington. They were all here now, everyone who had ever pretended to love her.

"He wasn't kidnapping me," she said. "I wanted to go with him." She looked at her mother. "I wanted to get away from her."

confession

Roni could hardly believe what happened next. The moment Alicia said she wanted to get away from her, Mrs. Thorn took two steps toward her daughter and hit her in the face so hard that Alicia fell to the ground.

Bill Camden launched himself toward his ex-wife, but Officer Spall grabbed him and slammed him back against the pickup truck.

Arnold Thorn stepped toward his wife, saying, "Now dear . . ."

Mrs. Thorn was bent over Alicia, her face contorted with fury, saying, "You worthless little tramp! You don't think of anybody but yourself! Do you ever think about me? No! All you want is to make out with your low-class boyfriend and make me look bad in front of my friends."

"You don't *have* any friends," Alicia muttered, looking up at her mother.

Mrs. Thorn drew back her hand to hit Alicia again, but Detective Bain—Brian's mother—grabbed her arms and twisted them behind her back.

Mr. Thorn helped Alicia to her feet. She was bleeding where her mother's red fingernails had raked across her cheek.

"Are you okay?" he asked.

"Yes," she said, shaking off his hand. "No thanks to you."

"I'm sorry, honey. I didn't know she was going to do that."

"You never know anything!"

"You know what Alice is like," said Bill Camden to Arnold Thorn. "You should have protected Alicia. I always did."

"I didn't want to get between mother and daughter," Thorn said.

"You're worthless," Camden snorted.

Mrs. Bain kept an arm on Alice Thorn and gave Arnold Thorn a careful look. "Are you saying that this has happened before?"

Arnold Thorn shook his head helplessly.

"It sure has," said Maurice, stepping forward. "Her mom was always smacking her around."

"That's a lie!" said Mrs. Thorn.

"Why didn't you say anything about this before?" Mrs. Bain asked.

"Alicia made me promise not to," Maurice said. "She said it would be too embarrassing for her family."

Mrs. Bain turned to Alicia. "Is that true, Alicia?"

Alicia shrugged.

"Last Friday, when you said you were attacked by a stranger, was it really your mother who hurt you?"

Alicia looked at her mother, who was glaring at her with eyes squeezed down to tiny slits.

"Alicia?" said Mrs. Bain. "Is that what happened?"

"Ask *him*." Alicia looked at her stepfather.

Arnold Thorn looked at his wife, then looked away, his face reddening.

"Yes," he said. "It's true."

Mrs. Bain frowned. "You knew this all along?"

"I knew that they had . . . had a fight. Maurice had stopped by to visit Alicia. Alice had made it clear to Alicia that Maurice was not welcome in our home. They had words."

"It was more than words," Maurice said.

Thorn nodded. "Yes. Alicia was hurt. I tried to help her, but she ran off. The next thing we knew she had told the police she had been attacked by a stranger." He spread his hands helplessly. "I didn't know what to do. I didn't want our family name to be dragged through the mud. We hoped it would all blow over."

"You are worse than worthless," said Bill Camden.

"And I suppose Alicia wasn't really abducted, either," said Mrs. Bain.

"No, that was real," said Arnold Thorn. "I'm certain Alice had nothing to do with that."

Roni couldn't hold herself back any longer. "We found the boat," she said.

Everyone turned and looked at her.

"Who is 'we'?" asked Detective Bain. She looked from Roni to Brian, who had been trying very hard to make himself invisible. "And what boat?"

"The boat Alicia was locked up on," Roni said. "The *Cap'n Arnold*."

"Alicia was on *your* boat?" Mrs. Bain said to Arnold Thorn.

"Actually, Mr. Thorn sold the boat to Maurice," Roni said.

Mrs. Bain turned her attention to Maurice.

"Is that true?"

Maurice shrugged.

Detective Bain looked at Officer Spall. "Maybe we should throw them *all* in jail."

"Look here," said Bill Camden, "I don't know anything about any boat. All I know is that Alicia isn't safe here in Bloodwater. Not with her around." He pointed with his chin at Mrs. Thorn.

"She's *my* daughter," shouted Mrs. Thorn.

Mrs. Bain turned to Alicia, who was sitting slumped over, looking as pale as a ghost. "Alicia, it's time to tell us what happened."

Alicia shook her head and moved closer to her father. Bill Camden put his arm around her. Roni was surprised by how small Alicia looked, as if she'd shrunk two sizes in one week.

"Alicia?" said Mrs. Bain.

Alicia shook her head.

"Tell them, Alicia," said Brian, stepping up next to Roni.

Alicia licked her lips, saying nothing.

"Talk to us, dear," said Mrs. Bain.

Alicia shook her head. "It was a stranger. I never saw him before. He locked me in the boat."

"Your dad's old boat? Your boyfriend's boat? Why didn't you tell the police whose boat it was?" Roni asked.

"I didn't . . . it was *dark!* I didn't know!"

"You had to know. The roses that Maurice gave you were in there," Roni pointed out.

Roni glanced at Maurice. His mouth was hanging open again. Not a good look. But not the look of a kidnapper about to be exposed, either. In fact, nobody looked particularly guilty. Even Mr. Thorn, peeking out from beneath his bandaged forehead, seemed more curious than worried.

"Tell them, Alicia," Brian said again. "Tell them what *really* happened."

What's Brian getting at? Roni wondered. What does he know? And why don't I know it, too?

Alicia lifted her head, giving Brian a pleading, I-can't-bring-myself-to-say-it look.

"We've seen the boat," Brian said. "The door was kicked in."

"I had to escape!" Alicia said, her voice small.

"But the door was kicked *in,*" Brian said. "You had to kick the door in from the outside. You broke the lock to get *into* the cabin. There was no way to lock you in!"

Alicia looked at her feet, saying nothing.

"Is that true, Alicia?" asked Detective Bain.

For several seconds, nobody said a word. Then Alicia looked up. She looked at her mother, and then at Maurice, and finally at her father.

"I'm sorry," she said. "I guess I snatched myself."

all you need is love

Everyone was looking at Alicia.

Alicia shrugged. "I didn't plan it. I just wanted to get away. The only place I could think to go was the boat. I wasn't going to stay away for long." She looked at Maurice. "I thought maybe Maurice would come. I thought he might look for me."

Maurice stared back at her with a confused expression on his face.

Alicia continued. "But he never came. I fell asleep. Then the storm came and the boat broke loose and I got thrown into the river and had to swim in the storm and I passed out and the next thing I knew it was the next day. I got lost trying to get home, and when I found out everybody thought I'd been abducted . . . I just thought maybe if I let them think that, then people would be nicer to me."

Alicia looked at her mother and touched a hand to the scratches on her cheek. Then she looked back at Maurice. "I didn't want to get anybody in trouble."

Everyone started talking at once. Brian couldn't take it all in, but it was exciting. Roni was giving him a weird look, but he was getting used to that.

Mrs. Thorn began shouting again. "How could you do

this to me? All you've ever wanted to do is make me look bad."

"That's not true!" said Alicia, her eyes overflowing with tears. "All I ever wanted was for you to stop hurting me and start loving me."

Mrs. Thorn dropped her eyes.

Mrs. Bain went back to the squad car and opened the back door. The thin man with the crewcut got out. He was wearing handcuffs. Mrs. Bain unlocked the cuffs and led him over to Alicia.

"I think you owe this man an apology," she said.

There was dead silence for a few moments, while everybody tried to puzzle out who this stranger could be and why Alicia should apologize to him.

"Who are you?" Alicia finally asked.

The man smiled. "My name is Douglas Unger," he said.

Roni and Brian both gasped. Driftwood Doug looked at them and winked.

It took Brian's mother another ten minutes to get everybody calmed down and off the street. Garth Spall seemed to think they should arrest somebody—but who? Eventually they decided to take Mrs. Thorn downtown. Roni overheard Mrs. Bain say to Spall, "Give her time to calm down and maybe talk to a family counselor."

Bill Camden wanted to take Alicia back to Mankato with him, but Mrs. Bain wouldn't allow it.

"My daughter will be safe with me," Camden said.

"We'll see that she's safe, but right now the Thorns have custody," said Mrs. Bain. "You will have to go through the courts to change that."

"Believe me, I will!" Bill Camden left in his pickup truck, which was seriously dented but still driveable.

Roni and Brian went over to Driftwood Doug, who was watching the drama with a little smile on his face. Without his hair and beard he looked more like an accountant than a wild woodsman.

"What happened to all your hair?" Brian asked.

"I thought nobody would recognize me without my hair and beard. But your mother spotted me walking down the street. She knew me from back when I lived in that cursed mansion." He smiled at Brian. "I guess being observant runs in the family."

"Roni and I never thought you were guilty," Brian said.

"I have to ask you one more thing," Roni said.

"Ask away," said Doug.

"Why did you run away from the police?"

Doug blushed. "I guess that wasn't very smart," he said. "It was the ginseng, you see."

"The ginseng made you run?"

"In a sense. You see, I'd been picking wild ginseng out of season and, well, I was afraid they'd come to arrest me for poaching."

"You mean we were drinking poached ginseng tea?"

"I'm afraid so." He looked over at Mrs. Bain, who was ordering Mr. Thorn and Alicia to return to Bloodwater

House. "You know, I think I'll head on back to my boat before your mother changes her mind about letting me go." He shook hands with Roni and Brian and said, "Thanks for believing in me. Stop by for a cup of tea next time you're in my neighborhood!" With that, he turned and walked away.

Mrs. Bain, watching Douglas Unger's long strides carry him quickly out of sight, said, "And to think I nearly put that poor man in jail!"

"That's what happens when you jump to conclusions," Brian said.

Mrs. Bain said, "Excuse me? Did I hear a voice?"

"I—"

"No," said Mrs. Bain. "I could not possibly have heard my son's voice, because *my* son is *grounded*!"

"But I—"

"In fact"—she rattled the handcuffs she had removed from Driftwood Doug's wrists—"if I were to get home and find that boy anywhere other than in his room studying, I might just cuff him to his bed rail for the rest of his sorry life." Mrs. Bain turned to Maurice. "If you happen to see my son, would you do me a favor and give him a ride home?"

"Uh . . . sure, I guess," said Maurice.

"And no detours!"

heroes

On the way home, Roni said, "I wonder who called the cops."

"That would be me," said Maurice. "When you took off in my truck I called 911 on my cell phone." He scowled at Roni. "You know who's going to pay for a new front bumper, right?"

"It was for a good cause," Roni said. "By the way, I have a question for you, Mr. Car-keyer. Are you the one who vandalized the *Cap'n Arnold*?"

Maurice shook his head. "That was Mrs. Thorn," he said. "She was jealous because Arnold was spending too much time on his boat. When she gets mad, she can go ballistic. I mean, you saw her. She got so mad she went down to Arnold's boat one day and just started busting stuff." He laughed. "It turned out to be a great deal for me—I got a good boat cheap."

Brian asked, "What happened that night at the Thorns'? The night Alicia got hurt."

"I went to see Alicia," Maurice said. "She'd broken up with me, but I had to talk to her one more time. It turned out she broke up with me because Mrs. Thorn thought I was too low class for her daughter. Alicia was all conflicted about her mom. She wanted her mom to love her, but at the same time she wanted to get away from her. I kept telling her she couldn't have both. We were out by the pool when Mrs. Thorn came out of the house, and then she and Alicia got into it. Alicia has a temper, too, you know."

"I know," said Roni, remembering getting whacked with Alicia's backpack.

"So they were yelling at each other, and all of a sudden Mrs. Thorn goes crazy on Alicia and starts hitting her."

"And you took off running," Roni said.

"How'd you know that?"

"We have our sources," Roni said.

Brian said, "What I don't get is why you let everybody think she'd been beat up by some stranger."

"Alicia called me later that night and made me swear to keep my mouth shut. She was worried it would make her family look bad." Maurice shrugged. "So . . . the *Cap'n Arnold* . . . you going to tell me where it is now?"

"It washed up on Nun's Island," Roni said.

"How's it looking? Is it in okay shape?"

Roni thought about the *Cap'n Arnold,* half full of bilge-water and rotting roses.

"It's in great shape, Maurice. It's just perfect."

"Now what?" Brian said to Roni.

Maurice, who was anxious to drive out to Nun's Island to check on his boat, had dropped them off on Main Street, a few blocks from their houses.

"Now we walk home and get dried off."

"We're almost dry already."

"Yeah, but we still smell like dead fish," Roni said, wrinkling her nose. "Time to go home, get cleaned up, then get grounded all over again."

"I thought the idea was that we'd be heroes and everybody would love us too much to punish us."

"Don't get your hopes up. The idea was that we would save Alicia from some evil kidnapper. But all we did was get her to admit she kidnapped herself. Oh, by the way, Stink Bomb, I owe you something."

"What?"

Roni made a fist and drove it into Brian's shoulder.

"Yowch!" Brian exclaimed, backing away and grabbing his arm. "What was *that* for?"

"For keeping me in the dark. How come you didn't tell me about the kicking-in-the-door thing?"

" 'Cause I didn't figure it out right away." He rubbed his arm. "Jeez!"

"I don't believe you. I think you knew it the whole time, ever since we were on the boat."

"I figured it out later, when we were going to see Maurice. I tried to tell you, but that's when you weren't talking to me. You told me to shut up. Besides, I didn't like when you were shoving me around on the boat."

"That was because you *scared* me."

"It was just a joke," Brian said.

"It wasn't funny."

They glared at each other for a few seconds. Then a big smile stretched across Brian's face.

"Yes, it was," he said, rubbing his shoulder and grinning. "Rat snakes," he said, then started laughing.

For about one-tenth of a second, Roni wanted to pummel the kid. But then something else rose up inside her and she was laughing, too.

54

lights out

It had been two weeks since Roni and Brian had cracked the Alicia Camden case, but they had not been hailed as heroes. In fact, things were much as before. Brian shifted position on The Bench. It got harder every time he sat on it. Mrs. Washington was hammering on her keyboard. A copy of last week's *Bloodwater Pump* sat on his lap.

Brian turned to the other occupant of The Bench. "So . . . what are you in for?"

"I was doing my job," Roni growled. "I wrote an article about Alicia snatching herself, and about how she has to do community service to make up for filing a false police report and wasting everybody's time, and how Mrs. Thorn has checked herself into an anger management program. But Spindler wouldn't let me run the story. He said it would be too embarrassing for Alicia and her family."

"I heard she and Ted were moving back to Mankato with their dad."

"They're going to stay with Arnold Thorn till the end of the semester. The Thorns are getting divorced and selling Bloodwater House. I think maybe Driftwood Doug is right about that place. Maybe there really is a curse."

"But how come they sent you down here?"

"I sneaked my article onto the school website. Didn't you see it?"

Brian shook his head. "I've been working on a physics project."

"Well, everybody else did. Spindler got pretty upset." Roni glanced at Mrs. Washington, then leaned toward Brian and said in a quiet voice, "I think he's going to have me tortured and killed."

"Sounds unpleasant," Brian whispered back.

"Yes, I was hoping for a simple execution. By guillotine, perhaps."

For a few seconds Brian and Roni contemplated death by guillotine and listened to the buzz of the fluorescent lights, the hum of the computer and printer, and the rattle of Mrs. Washington's fingers on the keyboard.

Roni said, "What about you?"

Brian shrugged. "I was making an electromagnet for physics class. Mr. Oppenheimer didn't like that I tapped into the school's emergency generator."

"You really did that?" Roni said.

"It wasn't that hard. I just hope when he disconnects it he knows enough to—"

All the lights in the school went out. For one entire second, there was silence—no buzzing lights, no humming computers, no rattling keyboard—then Mrs. Washington gasped. A muffled exclamation came from within Spindler's office.

Brian said, "Oops."

Turn the page for a preview of the next book in

THE BLOODWATER MYSTERIES:

skullduggery

1
bones

Dr. Andrew Dart had climbed thirty feet up the limestone bluff when a rock struck an outcropping just above his head. Dart flinched, then looked up. He saw and heard nothing.

Dart drew a shuddering breath. Chunks of limestone, loosened by wind and rain, sometimes broke away on their own. A few inches to the right and it could have killed him.

He rested on a shallow ledge and wiped his brow. From his perch he could see over the trees to where Bloodwater River flowed into the Mississippi. Not many wild places like this left in southern Minnesota.

All this land had once been populated by Native Americans. The rivers had been their freeways. They had built great villages looking out over the Mississippi River—maybe even right here, at the top of this rocky precipice.

The bluff he was climbing, and the woodland below, were now owned by Bloodwater College, where Dart was a professor of archaeology. But in a few days the land would be sold to a developer. Dart had taken it upon himself to do a final survey of the area before the bulldozers arrived. If he could find just one good piece of archaeological evidence—the ruins of a Native American village, or a burial mound—the college might be persuaded to stop the sale. Even a single unusual artifact might be enough.

Dart resumed his climb. Moments later, he had reached the odd cleft in the rock he had seen from below. There was a concealed opening, a crack in the bluff just wide enough for a man to squeeze through. He sniffed. Bat guano. A good sign there was a cave.

He stood in the entrance and tried to get a grip on himself. He hadn't planned on exploring a cave. All he had was the small flashlight attached to his key chain. And he did not like dark places. But this was important.

He forced himself to take a few steps into the cave, then stopped and let his eyes adjust to the dark. The passageway was narrow and low. He ducked his head and followed the weak beam of his flashlight. He felt panic rise in his chest as the passage narrowed. The rock walls seemed to be closing in on him, but he forced himself to move farther into the cavern.

The passageway soon widened into a large chamber. He could hear the chittering of bats from above. Staying close to the wall, he came upon another narrow passageway leading off to the right. He saw footprints in the dust—he was not the first person to visit this cave. As he examined a footprint, he heard a shuffling noise. He froze, listening carefully, but didn't hear it again. Probably an echo.

Moving deeper into the chamber, he gasped at what he saw next. A collection of dry yellow bones lay piled against the cavern wall.

A skeleton! Was it human? Yes! He could see the skull!

He shined his flashlight into the empty eye sockets. *This is just what I need!* he thought.

Dart heard the shuffling sound again. He turned to look just as something smashed into the back of his head. He pitched forward, and the last thing he heard was the snapping of ancient, brittle bones.

2
blue eyes

Roni Delicata stared at Professor Bloom's face with what she hoped might be mistaken for polite attentiveness. In fact, she was merely noting how much he looked like a lady's slipper orchid, with his pouchy lower lip, pink face, bulging eyes, and batlike ears. It made sense, Roni thought, since that was all the man seemed to want to talk about. Lady's slippers and trout lilies.

Yawn.

"The Bloodwater Bottoms is home to dozens of endangered wildflower species," the professor intoned, pointing to a map with his cane. "Not only lady's slippers and trout lilies, but also such rare beauties as *Latinus misbegottenus, Boringus dullemia,* and *Mesmerus dozingus . . .*"

Roni shook herself awake.

"Did you have a question, young lady?" said Professor Bloom.

"Um, no . . . I just wondered if, uh . . ." She tried to think of something—anything—interesting. "Are there any *poisonous* plants?"

"Indeed!" said the professor, rapping the hard wooden tip of his cane on the floor. "Certain mushrooms such as *Amanita virosa* and *Galerina autumnalis* can be deadly. And of course there is *Symplocarpus foetidus,* better known as skunk cab-

4

bage, which is toxic if not properly cooked. Also, the seeds of the native bindweed plant, a type of morning glory, produce a powerful hallucinogen. In addition, there are . . ." He went on with a list of long Latin names.

Looking out the corner of her eye, Roni noted that several of the other students were also struggling to stay awake. The only one who seemed at all interested was Brian Bain. That figured. Brian was fascinated by all things nerdy and scientific, no matter how boring. Fortunately, this character flaw was offset by the fact that Brian was also fascinated by explosive devices, clandestine operations, and other risky behaviors.

Brian caught her looking at him and stuck out his tongue. Roni looked away. So immature. But what could you expect? Sure, he was smart enough to have gotten bumped up to the ninth grade, but he was still just a kid.

Why had she signed up for this stupid Regional Studies class? It was the middle of the summer. She should be out having fun in the sun like practically every other kid in Bloodwater. But *noooooo*! Her mother, Nick, had decided that a perfect B-minus average was not good enough for a girl of Roni's "great potential."

Potential, schmotential. If this orchid-faced nutjob kept hammering her with Latin swamp-plant names, her brain would melt into a puddle of primordial ooze.

"Aren't we supposed to go on a field trip?" another student asked.

"Indeed we are! This afternoon we will be exploring the

Bloodwater Bottoms, one of the few areas of virgin forest remaining in the county—yes, young man?"

Brian asked, "Didn't I hear something about a housing development going up in the bottoms?"

The professor scowled. "A company called Bloodwater Development wanted to build a condominium complex right along the river, which would have permanently damaged the delicate ecosystem. Totally irresponsible!" As he spoke, the professor's face turned red. He pounded his fist into his palm. "They would have destroyed the last of the trout lilies!" He paused and took a deep breath. "Fortunately, the developers decided to build their condominiums on top of Indian Bluff, rather than in the precious bottomlands."

Professor Bloom frowned, looking toward the back of the room. "Excuse me, young man, are you registered for this seminar?"

Everyone turned to look at the boy who had just walked into the classroom.

Omigod, thought Roni.

She squeezed her eyes closed, then opened them. He was still there: tall and blue eyed with curly black hair. Omigod, she whispered to herself. Blue eyes and black hair did it to her every time.

The boy looked at the sheet of paper in his hand. His dark eyebrows came together in a way that made Roni's belly go all tingly.

"Is this Regional Studies?" the boy asked.

"Indeed it is," said Professor Bloom. "You are twenty-two minutes late."

"I got lost. We just moved to town last week and I—"

"Be that as it may, arriving late to the first day of class is not an auspicious beginning."

"A not a *what*?" said the boy.

A nervous laugh erupted from Roni's throat. She couldn't stop it. It sounded like a bullfrog belching.

She clapped a hand to her mouth, but it was too late. Every single person in the classroom—including *him*—turned and stared at her. She wanted to climb under her desk and die.

"Did you say something, Miss Delicata?" asked the professor.

Roni shook her head vigorously. Her face had to be the color of a beet. Gennifer Kohlstad, two rows over, gave her a knowing smirk. Roni looked away, going from embarrassed to furious. A gorgeous guy with blue eyes and black hair would also appeal to a tart like Gennifer. Roni wouldn't have a chance against Gennifer's sexy boy-killer looks and bubbly personality.

The professor returned his attention to the new student and directed him to the nearest desk.

"What is your name, son?"

"Eric." The boy smiled. "Eric Bloodwater."

3
curses

Bloodwater? Brian Bain twisted his neck to get a better look at the kid, who had sat at a desk near the back of the room. Eric Bloodwater leaned forward in his seat, as if looking attentive would make up for his late arrival.

Nobody named Bloodwater had lived in Bloodwater for nearly fifty years. And *those* Bloodwaters . . . well, they'd pretty much gone insane and killed each other off. In fact, every Bloodwater Brian had ever heard of had come to a bad end.

Some people said there was a Bloodwater Curse. Curse or no, the Bloodwaters were ancient history. Brian had always assumed that the whole clan had died out years ago.

But this kid did not look dead. Or cursed.

"Mr. Bain, would you mind directing your attention to the front of the room?" asked Professor Bloom.

"Sorry," Brian said, looking back at the professor.

"As I was explaining for Mr. Bloodwater's benefit, today we are studying the plant life endemic to Bloodwater Bottoms and the surrounding area. Later this week, Dr. Andrew Wyndham Dart will visit us to talk about Native American archaeology in the region. We will also learn about Bloodwater politics and government, which will include a visit to the county courthouse and jail.

"Now, as I was saying, a number of rare plant species can be found in the hardwood forests along the lower Bloodwater . . ."

Brian sneaked a look at Roni Delicata, a few rows over. He hadn't seen much of her lately. Actually, not since they'd gotten themselves in a world of trouble by investigating—and solving—the Alicia Camden kidnapping. That had been fun. Dangerous, but fun.

Brian wouldn't have minded hanging out with Roni more, but they didn't really have much in common. He was three years younger than her. He was smart about science stuff; she didn't care if the earth was round, flat, or triangular. She was a reporter for the school paper; he belonged to the Robot Club and the Chess Club. She was good at talking to people; he always stuck his foot in his mouth. About the only thing they had in common was that they both liked solving crimes. Without a crime, they just didn't have much to talk about.

Roni kept sneaking looks toward the back of the room. What was she looking at? Brian followed her glance and decided she was looking at Eric Bloodwater.

Uh-oh, he thought. That could mean two things.

Either she'd developed an instant crush, or she'd found herself another mystery.

Or both.

4

skunk cabbage

Professor Bloom said they'd head out for their first field trip after lunch to search for lady's slipper orchids, trout lilies, and skunk cabbage.

Skunk cabbage? Roni couldn't imagine why anyone would want to find such a horridly named specimen. She found a place to sit on the low brick wall outside the school and opened her container of peach yogurt. The yogurt was disgusting and the wall was uncomfortable, but she had a perfect view of Eric Bloodwater, who was sitting by himself with his back against the trunk of a small tree.

Maybe she should go over and sit down next to him. Ask him a really interesting question to show him how smart and fascinating she was. Either that or just smile and simper and gaze at him adoringly, which was what most guys seemed to want.

Roni forced down another spoonful of the sickeningly sweet peach yogurt. She had an olive loaf sandwich in her bag, but she didn't want Eric to see her shoving a huge sandwich down her throat. The yogurt seemed more elegant.

She stole another look at Eric Bloodwater and sighed. He was just *too* good-looking. She didn't have a chance. Not unless she instantly dropped fifteen pounds. And her legs grew a couple of inches. And . . . what was she thinking? She was who she was. Roni Delicata, teenage shlump.

On the other hand, she had nothing to lose. If he told her to get lost, at least she could stop thinking about him. Maybe.

"Whatcha staring at, Sherlock?"

Roni jumped.

"Don't *do* that!" she snapped at Brian, who had sneaked up behind her. She gave him her best glare, but Brian, in his eternal Brianly way, didn't seem to notice. He sat down on the wall beside her, his broad, open, Korean face smiling.

"Isn't this class great?" he said.

"Sure, if you like being bored out of your skull. I'm not here by choice."

"You flunk a class?"

Roni looked around, making sure that no one else could hear her. "No, I didn't flunk anything, but my mom thought my grades could be improved."

"Cool."

"No, Brian, it isn't cool. It's pathetic. I have much more important things I could be doing with my summer."

"Name one."

"How about sleeping till noon? Instead of tramping around in the woods looking for skunk cabbage. You don't think he's gonna make us eat it, do you?"

Brian laughed. "You kidding? *Symplocarpus foetidus* is poisonous!"

"You spout one more Latin name I'm going to pour this yogurt over your head."

Professor Bloom appeared at the door of the school. He hung his cane over his forearm and clapped his hands.

"People! People! Gather 'round, please!"

Brian and Roni walked up to him together. He pointed at them. "You two are a pair." Then he proceeded to pair off the rest of the class. To Roni's horror, he put Gennifer with Eric.

"We will be using the buddy system when we're in the bottoms this afternoon. Stick with your partner and try to avoid sinkholes, bogs, stinging nettles, poison ivy, rattlesnakes, and other potential sources of discomfort. You will each be assigned a particular species, choosing from the list of plants I handed out at the beginning of class. Think of it as a sort of scavenger hunt."

Brian's hand shot up. "Can Roni and I have skunk cabbage?"

Roni felt her face turning pink. Why had she let the little twit even walk next to her? Now she was stuck with him—and skunk cabbage—for the rest of the day.